Encyclopocalypse Publications
www.encyclopocalypse.com

Jesse D'Angelo

SPECIAL THANKS

Sherri Sellers McCune
Tracey Nudd
Max Tackett
Sean Duregger
Sarah DeRosa
Niq Wittig
And my lovely wife, Lauren
For putting up with me
You rock

CONTENTS

CHAPTER 1

I WATCH as Larry Lindner melts some cunt's eyeballs out of her head.

I'm at home, folding laundry and sipping whiskey as the new clash plays on the big screen. I could be at the arena right now, watching The Boogey-Man Championships live with everyone else, but fuck that. I don't need to bump into Larry in the hallways and hear him brag about how he's the champion, he's the best, blah blah blah. I mean, he's *good,* and I have to admit I'm a little jealous of the shit he can do.

This bitch thinks she can hide from him in the bathroom, but then there he comes, Larry "The Snapper," floating through the fucking walls. She screams in confusion and agony as Larry works his magic, and it *is* magic. At first, she feels a warmth in her optic nerves, which grows into unbearable heat. Her eyeballs begin to swell and throb, then finally pop like zits. Molten blood and goo melts down her cheeks. She screams real good.

Larry sits on the toilet, his legs crossed, twiddling his thumbs.

"What's the matter?" he asks. "Can't believe your eyes?"

The audience in the arena bursts into laughter and applause.

I roll my eyes, down the rest of my drink, and

continue with my laundry. Bastard. I can't do shit like that. He made one guy think insects were all over him and let the fucker scratch himself to death. He turned this one bitch's tongue into a snake which of course proceeded to bite her to death. He can fly, walk through walls, fuck with reality. And he's a smartass with a flair for dramatics who's evil and sadistic and excels at torture. *And* his fucking head has been flayed of all skin, and iron bear-trap teeth are bolted onto his jaws.

I'm just big and strong.

Stop it, Marvin, don't get down on yourself. I'm not just big and strong, I'm seven feet tall-three hundred and fifty pounds-big and strong. And my face is a gnarled mess thanks to my botched suicide attempt years ago after murdering my family. My whole mouth has been reconstructed and my nose is just gone. So I am a very big, very strong and very ugly redneck who loves to murder and inflict pain. And I like to think that I bring a certain style and flare to what I do. I've got charm and personality. *I* should be champion!

Larry follows his mortified victim as she stumbles into her bathtub. Screaming for help, she flails wildly as her empty eye sockets continue to ooze. Larry chuckles, holding up his hand and making a motion like sprinkling spices. At his psychic command, Larry's victim convulses. Looks like she needs to take a big shit. But a turd isn't what comes out of her. At first it looks like she shits out a bunch of black oil, but the mass is moving. When they cut in closer I can see it's fucking cockroaches.

Big and small, brown and black, lots and lots of cockroaches.

And they're not just coming out of her asshole, it's clear that these fuckers are bursting from every orifice they can find. Soon her screams are silenced as she starts barfing live cockroaches and choking on them. Roaches gushing out of her cunt. Roaches ripping through her belly button. Her nose. Her ears. They scuttle and slither out of her vacant orbital sockets, and her body spasms as the sea of creepy crawlies tear her apart from the inside out. It's actually quite beautiful.

Larry stands up and takes a bow. The crowd goes wild.

Fuck. How am I supposed to compete with *that?*

I mean, I have to admit, that gave me a little chubby. That was good. Fuck. But whatever, I'm Marvin fucking Brumlow. The biggest and the baddest, baby. I'll figure something out. But in the meantime, as much as I fucking *hunger* to dethrone that skinny bastard and put the belt around *my* waist, I have other concerns. Suspicions. Something is not right and I don't fucking know what it is.

So I started profiling my former victims in my free time. Which is pretty much all the time when I'm not doing my thang. I've gone through the dossiers of the victims from my first two clashes again and again. I've realized they don't tell me very much. For each target, there is one photo and a one-page description. Just a few paragraphs and that's it. Where they're from, what they do, what they like... I don't know what I'm looking for. Something. *Something* more.

Why? I don't know. Back when I was alive, before I was executed and sent to Hell and turned into a superstar killing machine, I would prey on my victims with zero regard. Some teenage runaway at a truck stop? Dead. Some asshole who cut me off in traffic? Dead. Some nice yuppie being friendly and respectful and giving me no reason to wish him harm? Dead. I never gave a shit about any of them. Never checked their IDs, never dug into their lives, never needed more.

Now everything's different.

Now I'm famous and it's making me paranoid. And since I'm rich and have nothing to lose, I'm going to see where this rabbit hole takes me. In the meantime, my general afterlife plans remain the same: Get the belt, make increasingly more money, live like a king. If David Black is trying to screw me over somehow or set me up, I'll find out and make him pay through the ass. Burn the fucking BMC to the ground. Whatever he's up to, whatever they're not telling me, I'm gonna find out. I'm waiting on a very important delivery tonight, something that will hopefully shed some light.

I turn off the TV and toss the remote onto my two king-size beds pushed together setup. Can't stand to look at Larry's ugly mug anymore. Finishing off my drink, I glance around at my luxury apartment and nod in satisfaction. Well, almost satisfaction. I look at the clock on the wall. Almost eleven. My guest should be here soon.

I pour another drink and relax, walk around, dance in my flowing silk robe, take a shit. Things continue like this for a while and I'm getting antsy. Where the fuck is this little troll? I do not like being made to wait.

As I pace and clench my fists and visualize various methods of horribly murdering my unfortunate delivery boy, I finally hear the bell ring. Ah, good. I buzz him in and wait for my goodies like a dog being served a fat steak.

There's one more thing I want to do before my guest arrives, so I go into my bedroom to finish preparing. On my bedside table is a nice wooden box with a brass clasp. I open it up and behold my two new best friends.

Resting in a green-felt bedding are two custom dental implants, one for each jaw. A stainless steel construction holds together various molded plastics and ceramic teeth, designed specifically to fit into my mouth and fill in the gaps where my natural teeth and jaw bones no longer exist. They cost a small fortune, but I'm fucking rich now, so there you go.

I pick up the lower prosthetic and click it into place in my mouth. Ah, feels good. Snap the upper piece into position. Nice. Having these babies in makes it so much easier for me to speak and for others to understand me. It also makes me look better, with a proper jaw structure, so now my face doesn't look quite as much like an old man's diseased, wrinkly nut sack. I'm still scarred and hideous, but this is a lot better. I look at the mirror and smile. Look at those big, sparkly-white chompers!

Finally, I hear a knock at the front door.

There's my buddy, Snapdragon.

"Hey, Marvin," he says.

He has his usual puffy, uneven mohawk, his coke-bottle glasses, his street urchin, gutterpunk clothes. The little dude smiles nervously.

"You're late," I growl. Man, my voice is just a thing of beauty.

"S-Sorry. I was at the BMC clash. I came right over."

I step aside and let him in.

"Well?" I ask. "You got it or what?"

"Uh, well yeah. Sort of..." he says, pulling off his backpack. "Wow, the new teeth look great, man!"

"What do you mean, sort of?" Now I'm getting angry.

"I-I did what you said. I used the travel app and went to Earth, tried to dig up as much information as I could about your former victims." Snapdragon pulls a very slim manilla folder out of his bag. "Well as you know, I can't stay on the other side of the veil longer than an hour before I really risk getting detected. So I went in a couple times, tried to find as much as I could, but..."

"Just get to the point."

"Point is there's not much. With only an hour each time I go in, I can't exactly go research every single person you killed during one of your clashes. So I picked only a couple, the ones who supposedly lived close by, the ones I might find something on."

"And?"

"And really... nothing. I went to the Westport Main library, looking for newspaper clippings about the murders and victims. According to his dossier, Preston Edgecombe was supposedly from Westport, but I couldn't find any record of him. Same for Natasha Grant. When I find articles about the killings, the victims are always mentioned as 'unidentified.' So I don't know!"

I open the folder and there's nothing but a few scant newspaper clippings.

"That doesn' make sense," I say.

"You're telling me! When I was in Preston Edgecombe's home town, I went to the library, the town hall. Nothing. Couldn't find his name anywhere. I did find this one missing person clipping but it's from another county and the name is all wrong. Look," he points out the clipping, a short article headed by a blurry black and white photo of a young man with long hair. "See? Brian Cobb. Age twenty-seven. Disappeared without a trace. Looks a lot like Preston, doesn't it?"

It does resemble my favorite yuppie kill from that first clash, but the stats are all wrong. Preston was only eighteen, if memory serves, and he definitely wasn't from Westport. He was not twenty-seven years old with long hippie hair and a scruffy goatee. The man described in the article was basically a bum. A small-time criminal, drifter, occasionally working some menial job, no family to speak of. He'd disappeared, a brief missing person's report had been filed... and promptly forgotten. Nobody cared.

Nope, this was not my boy. Not Preston with his rich parents, clean-shaven style, fancy car, house on a lake, and white sweater tied around his fucking shoulders. This does not help me at all. No new information on Preston or anyone else.

Snapdragon clears his throat 3d holds out a trembling hand.

I glare at him and growl.

"Hey man," he says, "don't shoot the messenger."

Wouldn't dream of it. Don't want to get blood on my new rug.

"You kep' me waitin' for *this?*" I grab him by the lapels of his shitty jacket and lift him off the floor. His little chicken legs flail and kick.

"M-Marvin, please! I did what you said! I went in, I did the research! I-I can always do more! I can keep looking, keep digging! You want me to...?"

I deflate and lower him to the floor. He's telling the truth. Damn it. Now I have more questions than answers. And now I have Snapdragon looking up at me with his poor, pathetic, puppy dog-eyes. I did promise him a treat. So I reach into my pocket and pull out a wad of cash wrapped in a rubber band.

My little friend trembles as he holds out his hand, not sure if I'm going to pay him or rip his arm off. Honestly, I'm considering doing both just for a bit of novelty and fun. But Snapdragon has proven useful and I may need his services in the future. So I hand him the money.

"Keep diggin'," I say and push him out the door.

CHAPTER 2

JIM and I sit across from David Black.

I'm casual-cool today, donning a red and white Adidas track suit and a fat gold chain around my neck. Oh, and my new chompers, of course. Still barefoot, but oh well, just call me a Hobbit, I guess. Jim has chosen to wear the baggiest and most obnoxiously colorful shirt he could find, tucking it into black slacks, and accenting the whole look with one of those skinny ties. His greasy-black hair is pulled into a messy ponytail and, as always, he's chewing gum. Grape today, from the smell of it. Ugh.

Mr. Black sits at his desk in a simple black t-shirt and jeans. He taps his fingers on the desk, swiveling back and forth as he waits for Jim to finish reading my new contract. Line by line, my sleazy manager pores over the document, humming to himself as he chews, *smack smack smack*. Read faster, Jim.

Standing behind Mr. Black and lined up in front of the windows are four large security guards in black suits. Not as big as me, of course, but that goes without saying. Guess after our last meeting in here, when I murdered famed French footwear designer Henri Pantouffleé, Mr. Black is taking no chances with me. Not like these cunts could stop me anyway if I wanted to do something.

Maybe he knows I'm on to him. Or am I? I mean, I know something fishy is going on, but I don't know what, or who's responsible. Right now, I'm just soaking up information, keeping my eyes and ears open. I'm going to get to the bottom of this, and if Mr. Fancy-ass president of the BMC has been fucking me somehow, he's gonna get it in the ass sideways. I'll burn the whole fucking thing to the ground.

Jim finishes reading and clears his throat.

"Better?" Mr. Black asks.

"Not enough," Jim says, tossing the stapled document back onto the desk between them. "Not what we asked for. Come on, Dave." At the president's irritated expression, Jim drops his casual tone. "I mean, David. Uh, Mr. Black. Sir."

"You wanted more money, there's more money," Mr. Black says, his polished, bald head gleaming. "You're asking for the sun and the moon. Not gonna happen."

"We just want—"

"You want to make more than Larry Lindner makes," Mr. Black finishes for him. "*Not* gonna happen. Larry is our champion, our biggest draw."

"Well, Marvin should be the—"

"*I* should be the champion," I say, cutting Jim off. "I'm more popula' than Snappa' now. I killed more people in my last clash than him. I ain' relyin' on stupid gimmicks or magic powers, neither. I'm all-American meat n' potatas, baby. I'm the real deal and people know that."

"You've also only had two clashes. Tommy Torture and Bonecrusher have both been here longer than you. What about their title shot? You don't just become the BMC champion right away like that. You have to earn it."

"And how exactly do I do that?" I ask. "It's not like this is a sport with clearly defined rules."

"Who sells out every single show?" Black asks. "Who gets us the highest pay-per-view numbers? Whose merchandise sells the best? Who consistently kills every single one of his targets with amazing panache and creativity? That would be Larry 'The Snapper' Lindner, got it? When you've been here as long as him, and you never fail in taking out a target, and your numbers are better than his, then we'll talk. Meantime, you're living in the lap of fucking luxury; nice clothes, got yourself some nice, new teeth. You've got it made. Be happy with that."

"Still don't have a pair of shoes that fit me."

"You're on your own with that one now, Marvin. You want some custom shoes made, I think you can afford it," Mr. Black says, exasperated. "Meantime, here are the targets for your next clash," he says, tossing a folder onto the desk for me.

Jim snatches it up first, doing his due diligence as manager and scanning through the folder quickly. He mumbles, "Mm hm, mm hm" and smacks away at his gum as he reads. His expression sours and he looks up at the bossman, confused.

"This is an urban setting," Jim says. "Marvin is a rural kind of killer."

I snatch the folder away from Jim and begin to read. It's true, I'm always best in the country or other places where there aren't too many people. I need to be able to hide behind trees and bushes. Put me in an urban setting and I stand out like a sore fucking thumb.

"Look at the date," Mr. Black says with a smile.

I scan the pages and find it.

"October 31st?" I say.

"That's right! We're sending you in on Halloween night! Our darling little victims are all going to a costume dance party. And guess who will blend right in with all the vampires and werewolves and ghouls?"

I grunt and keep reading. I flip through the dossiers of victims, noting that there are only six of them this time. I'm confused.

"Only six?"

"What?" Jim chimes in, leaning to look at the folder in my hands. "Last time we had eight, right?"

"So what?" Mr. Black says. "He can always pick off some other random victims who pop up along the way. He always does."

Jim and I share a look. I shrug.

"So," Mr. Black asks, "do we have a deal?"

JIM AND I RIDE THE ELEVATOR BACK DOWN TO THE parking garage.

Some poor, random schmuck is in here with us, some wormy, mid-level exec type of cunt. He's got himself pressed as far into the corner as possible. Jim pops a new piece of gum and zealously begins to chew. *Smack smack smack.* I wonder what he does with his gum when he eats actual food? Does he sleep with gum in his mouth?

I open up the dossier file and flip through it again.

"Don't worry, man," Jim smacks. "I won't let that shark screw you over. The contract is solid. Let's just bide our time, play our cards right. Just keep kickin' ass, we'll get you that belt. Me, I got my eye on this little bungalow up in Babylon Hills. Get me some nice clothes, maybe that new Astin Martin... Yeah, baby."

I grumble, still focused on the dossier.

"What's up?" Jim asks.

"Somethin's just not... I don' know."

I want to tell Jim everything, voice my suspicions. But what is it that I even suspect? And what if Jim is in on it? Shit, anyone could be in on it. This is David Black, I'm sure he has eyes and ears everywhere. Even in an elevator. I remember that Jim and I are not alone and turn to look at our suited companion in the corner.

The little businessman trembles, trying to remain perfectly still. He's gripping his briefcase, looking at the floor, hoping to make himself invisible. When he feels me glaring at him, he timidly looks up. He smiles nervously, trying to look casual and relaxed.

"H-hi, Mr. Brumlow," he says.

Is he a spy? Shit, no way to know. Oh well, can't take any chances.

"Sorry," I say to the little man as I turn to face him.

I wrap my hand around his face and smash his head into the stainless steel corner, pulverizing his skull and sending all those beautiful tissues and fluids squirting through the mangled flesh of his face. Jim squeals and jumps back as blood and brains erupt against the wall of the elevator like a ruptured calzone and the twitching, headless body falls to the floor.

"Dude, what the fuck!" Jim screams.

"Sorry," I say. "Can't take any chances."

I look down at my hand, now covered in thick,

viscous blood and brains. Don't want to get any on my nice clothes. Shit, didn't think that one through. Oh well, fuck it, sorry Jim. I slap my gooey hand onto Jim's chest and proceed to wipe my hand clean on his shirt.

"*Oh, come on, Marvin!! What the fuck!!*"

"Sorry," I repeat as we reach the garage and the door opens. "He may have been spyin' on us."

"Spying? That was Marty Cohen from HR! Why would he have been spying? What are you talking about, man?"

Jim and I head into the garage, leaving the headless body behind to stew in its own shit. I look around and see nothing but cars. Good. Finally feeling we're alone, I stop and turn to face Jim.

"Somethin's goin' on," I say. "Somethin's up. Do you know anythin' about that?"

"Yeah, you're a fucking lunatic, Marvin! That's what's up!"

"I mean it, Jim. Somethin' doesn' feel right. Like the whole thing is fixed."

"Fixed how?"

"I don' know. Yet. Like, I dunno... Like the victims are all actors, or somethin'. Or the whole thing is fake, like they're all just video game characters. Like, it looks and feels like I'm killin' 'em, but really there's nobody there?"

"No, Marvin. That doesn't make any sense," Jim shakes his head, annoyed at me. "These kids are all real flesh and blood, dude. What do you think is dripping all over you when you step back through the veil after a clash? Real blood and guts! Come on, man!"

"Well, maybe it's not that, but it's somethin'. *Some-*

thin' is off here." I step closer, looking Jim in the eye, trying to be intimidating. "So I'll ask one more time, do you know anythin' about that?"

"No, I don't. Okay? And stop trying to scare me, Marvin. You hurt me, you hurt yourself. Remember?"

I grunt.

"Now, if you don't mind," Jim says, heading back to his little red convertible, "I'm gonna go home and throw this *five-hundred-dollar* shirt away and wash all this fucking *blood and brains* off of me! And you, young man, have your next clash to prepare for! So I suggest you go home and get some rest! Okay?"

"Fine."

"*Got it?*"

"Yeah yeah, fine."

I fucking hate Jim.

CHAPTER 3

I'M in my happy place.

At home. In my favorite chair by the fireplace. My Japanese silk robe. Bob Seger coming through the speakers. A glass of fine brandy. The lights of downtown Malavista sparkling through the wall of windows behind me. I've got my big 'ol feet up as I open the folder given to me by Mr. Black and begin to flip through the dossier of my new victims for the umpteenth time. However, this time I'm reading with a more discerning eye and I also have the dossiers of my last two clashes beside me. I'm asking questions, looking for patterns, but so far I'm coming up short.

First on the list to be horribly murdered is Richard. Another yuppie asshole. A junior at UC Berkeley, star tennis player, thinks his shit don't stink. I know the type. Puffy brown hair, skinny legs, fucking sweater tied around his shoulders. There's a brief history of where he went to school, what family he comes from, a basic background listed just like everyone else. I usually just skim past that shit, but now I'm paying closer attention, looking to see if anything stands out. But nope, nothing that turns on a lightbulb over my head and makes me say, "There's something fishy about this!"

Next up is Noelle. Hm, nice name. Looks like a nice girl, too. Long reddish-brown hair, valedictorian, book-club president, does community service at homeless shelters, helps find homes for orphaned animals. I don't care about any of that, I'm trying to check out that body of hers. In the photo, her clothes are not revealing at all. Baggy pants, puffy shirt buttoned up, so no cleavage, shoulder pads... I fucking hate the 80's. In any case, little Noelle here is anything but a slut or a bad girl who deserves to die, but who says "deserve" plays into this at all? This is a game, baby. I read the rest of her bio, and it vaguely mentions that she and Richard are in a relationship.

Huh? Are they or aren't they?

It looks like they used to be but are now at different schools, have taken time off but are now back together, sort of. This sounds eerily familiar. I think back to my last clash and it was the same thing with Johnny and Natasha. Two people with a vague history together who see each other after a long break and are kinda-sorta back together, but she's taking her time and isn't sure... very familiar. But does that mean anything or am I just thinking too hard? People do have complicated relationships, right? Hm. I keep reading.

Next on the list is Parker. Fat and obnoxious, Jew-fro, theater major, aspiring stand-up comedian. Great. Seems like every group has one like this. What's he doing here? Looks like he's been set up on a blind date for this upcoming Halloween party. Otherwise, there's a brief mention of him being friends with Richard, but that's it. Okay, pretty thin for a fat boy. Not much to go on... as usual.

I turn the page and I see Stephanie. Hello, Barbie!

This tall, lean little gazelle is picture fucking perfect. Long blonde hair, blue eyes, perfect makeup, perfect clothes, designer shoes. A little fashionista. A brief mention of her family and school history tells me nothing and there are no special hobbies or skills listed. I guess when you're this gorgeous, you can just be a fashion model or a trophy wife to some millionaire and that in itself is a special skill. Right? I chuckle as I read that little Stephanie is the intended blind date for Parker. Yeah, great idea! Somebody thought these two would hit it off??

I look at the next lucky contestant and smile. Kareem smiles back at me. At 6'4" and built like a brick shithouse, it looks like Kareem was a star linebacker in high school and is now a star college player. He and his girlfriend have the distinct honor of being my first Black victims in the BMC! *Finally* I get to kill some Black people! Oh man, they die sooo good! I'm looking forward to this one. Kareem is handsome and muscular, has a short little jheri-curl hairdo and is cocky as hell. Alpha male. Perfect, one of my favorite kinds of assholes to destroy.

His girlfriend, Missouri, or Mo for short, looks like she was plucked right out of central casting. She is the prototypical ghetto-fabulous Black woman. Doesn't go to school, doesn't have any skills—unless you count sucking Kareem's cock—and is generally loud, nasty, stupid and incredibly entitled. In the photo she's wearing what must be a wig, just a terrible, straight-maroon mop that's obviously not her real hair. Oh, she's *really* not gonna like getting slaughtered. Black people, for whatever reason, really *really* do not appreciate being horribly murdered, but that just increases my pleasure even more. Hey, I'm not racist. I hate everyone equally.

Still, Mo is just such a stereotype. They all are, really. There's just not much to any of them. A brief history of family and education, a list of hobbies and activities, a photo, and that's it. Not that I care to know them deeper, nor do the BMC fans at home or in the arena. Nobody wants a rich backstory for any of these muppets. They just want to see them run and scream and get gutted like fish. But still, the more I do this job, the more I can't help but wonder...

Why are all these kids even friends? These don't seem like people who would actually hang out together. Why would Parker and Stephanie get set up like this? Why would Richard even be friends with a loser like Parker to begin with? Why would Kareem and Mo even hang out with these stupid crackers at all? Why is there always some vague romantic relationship? I can't pin anything down, and obviously these are all different people than the ones from my previous clashes, but still... why do they all feel the same? The same, but different. So weird!

I've read through the dossier a dozen times and I'm still not coming up with anything. So I chug the rest of my brandy and stand up, feeling nice and warm and fuzzy. I dance and twirl to the music, moving from one room of my opulent penthouse to the next, reveling in my new life as a high roller.

I open my walk-in closet and run my fingertips across the racks of fine garments. I have custom-made suits, ties, cufflinks, you name it. Well, I still don't have any shoes.

Can't find a shoemaker in Hell who can make me a decent custom pair. I mean, there are a few who could, but after hearing about what I did to Henri Pantoufleé, none of them want to work with me. Whatever, barefoot is fine. My feet are so calloused I could walk over sharp rocks and broken glass and not even feel it. Still, I don't like my feet getting wet and cold, and it's so easily to slip in a puddle of blood. But whatever, barefoot is fine.

On one rack hangs my kill clothes. I now have six identical pairs of overalls hanging in a row. They're all custom made and weathered to look beaten up and dirty, so when one is utterly destroyed and caked in blood, piss, puke, cum, and grape jelly, I can just toss it and move on to the next. Ahhh, I love this new life. Afterlife. I cherish the privilege to be able to continue killing and killing, the adoration of the fans, the money... I don't think that could ever get old. Still, something's not quite right about this whole thing and I'm gonna get to the bottom of it.

CHAPTER 4

IT'S TIME.

I'm standing at those big double doors at the arena. Jim stands to my right and my corner team—Turi and the other two guys whose names I always forget—stand to my left, ready with a bucket, water and towels. I can not only hear, I can *feel* the crowd on the other side. Cheering, stomping their feet. I hear the booming voice of Bruno Bivens distorted and echoing through the arena's speakers. Getting them hyped up for me.

I stretch and flex these old muscles. I shift from foot to foot, getting antsy. Let me out there already! My overalls and wifebeater are appropriately dirty. My gorgeous new teeth are perfectly straight and sparkling white. Did I remember to take my magnesium this morning? Oh whatever, it's fine.

Jim slaps his hand on my back, trying to be encouraging or supportive, I guess. I give him a hard scowl and he withdraws the gesture, clearing his throat. Soon Bruno's intro reaches critical mass, his voice soars and he finally says —

"Ladies and gentlemen! The one, the only... MARVIN BRUMLOOOOOW!!!"

The doors fly open and the light of fame hits my face.

Ahhhh. The crowd erupts into thunderous applause.

I spread my arms wide like a murderous hillbilly

messiah and step into the spotlight. My walk-out song begins to play. *Bad Moon Rising*. Yeah, baby. I strut down the aisle as John Fogerty gleefully warns all the poor little sheep about the dangers of the night. Colorful lights and giant TV monitors. Signs saying things like "I love you Marvin" and "Kill 'em all, Marv!" The smells of popcorn and hotdogs and perfumes and armpits. Ahhh, I love this place. I'm king here. Well, maybe not quite yet.

As I begin to pass the table where the clash commentators sit, I notice that the special guest tonight is none other than my good buddy, Larry Lindner. Fuck. He's sitting there behind a microphone, wearing some kind of feathery pimp-suit made from pink angora and rhinestones. Ugh, I hate this fucking guy so much. I see him talking to the two other commentators but can't hear what they're saying. However, when Larry sees me his demeanor changes. He turns to face me and projects his voice, making sure I can hear him.

"And there he is," Larry says. "A sack of potatoes with feet."

I stop in my tracks and turn to face him.

"Excuse me?" I say, stalking up to their broadcast table.

"I think you heard me. Funny, I keep hearing about how you think you're gonna steal my title, take my belt. You do know there are levels to this game, right? And you are nowhere near my level, dough boy."

"Oh yeah, you wanna dance, pizza face? Let's go!"

Jim and my corner team do their best to hold me back, as do the people sitting around Larry. He's up on his feet in an instant, trying to get in my face.

"Fine! Show me how you dance with those two big left feet!"

"I'll rip that stupid bear trap off your mouth and shove it down your throat!"

"The Jaws of Death are my calling card," Larry says, gesturing to the iron fangs bolted to his skull. "They are ugly and menacing, the stuff of nightmares. What's that you got in your mouth, Marvin? Bunch of big-white fucking Chicklets? Yeah man, reeeaaal scary!"

Oh, that's it. Nobody talks shit about my new chompers.

I lunge at him.

"Marvin, stop!" Jim screams and tries to pull me back.

It seems like everyone in the arena piles on to pull us apart. All I see is a blur of hands, faces, shoulders, lights. Through it all I see his face. Larry is only inches away, looking me right in the eye. His eyes are an intensely crystal-clear blue — really quite beautiful, actually — and somehow, even under those big, iron jaws, I can tell he's smiling. Bastard.

This heaping mess continues for a minute before enough poor bastards squeeze between us and create some distance. I realize that this is not the time or place, so I allow Jim and the boys to pull me back. I'm still talking shit though, of course, acting like I want to go right now.

But honestly, I don't know how I'd even fight Larry! The guy is a fucking wizard! He could turn my fingers into hot dogs! He could turn me inside out! But can he do all that in Hell, or does he only have those powers on

Earth during a clash? Does he have any weaknesses I can exploit? Hmm. I'll figure something out. I'll find a way to beat this asshole.

"Good luck, Marvin!" Larry shouts as I walk away. "Have a great clash! Knock 'em dead, slugger!"

Oh, I'll be seeing you around, Snapper. Don't you worry.

I approach the stage. Turi holds up the water bottle for me and I take a sip through the straw. I roll my shoulders around a couple times, stretch my neck. Jim gives me a reassuring slap on the shoulder.

"This is it, big boy," he says. "Go do what you do. Just remember to have fun."

"And you," I say, leaning down and looking him in the eye. "You keep your eyes open, Jim. Let me know if you see anythin', hear anythin'. Remember..."

"I know, I know," Jim says. "Something weird is going on. Got it."

I growl at him. He stops chewing his gum for a second, takes a deep breath, and his face softens, like he's going to at least try to take my request seriously.

"Fine," he says. "I got it. Now go. Do horrible things."

I smile and slap his shoulder. The stage beckons. I scale the staircase in three long strides, stepping up onto the stage and looking around at all the thousands of faces around me. The lights. The music. The dancing girls, *well helloooo*. There's my favorite hummingbird buddies, the eight drone cameras that follow me around for my clashes. There's Bruno Bivens waiting for me center stage in a glittery, gold suit, the glowing gate to another world right behind him.

I hold my arms out and spin around to everyone's delight.

Sparks fly. Angels sing. Everyone loses their shit.

I have a job to do and I'm gonna do it. But this time there's more. Yes, I'm gonna hack these kids up real good, of course, but I have my own secret mission as well. I'm keeping my eyes and ears open, and I'm asking questions. Detective Marvin Brumlow. That's right, I'm getting to the bottom of whatever the fuck is going on.

Tucked in the breast pocket of my overalls is a small note pad and a ballpoint pen. In another pocket is a protein bar. Hey man, sometimes you need a snack. Otherwise, I've had the foresight this time to bring with me a stopwatch, which is set to Hell-time. The alarm is set to go off at my mandated breaks, where I'm rudely yanked out of Earth reality and back into the arena. This way I can check on my time and not be randomly pulled out of it when I'm not expecting. Brilliant, right?

That's all I'm taking with me. No cheesy mask, no weapons, just me. Well, I do have one weapon with me, but I'm not planning to use it the way one would think. It's a nice little Smith & Wesson .38 special. Loaded with dummy rounds. I've been thinking about a really sweet kill, and if I set it up just right and pull it off... oh yeah, baby. It's gonna be a good one. Tee-hee.

"MAR-VIN! MAR-VIN!!"

I flex my muscles and scream like a monster.

"Marvin, are you ready?" Bruno shouts into the mic.

I roar and approach that billowy veil, looking around at the crowd. Jim and my crew. David Black. Larry Lindner. Satan. Other boogeymen like Bloody Mary and

Preying Mantis. Bonecrusher. Snakebite. Bob Franks. Hey, not everyone has a cool name, but everyone is here to watch me slice and dice. Well, I'm ready, motherfuckers. Let's party.

"Then the time... has come... *TO KILL!!!*"

Everyone goes apeshit as the buzzer goes off and first period starts.

I fucking jump through the veil.

CHAPTER 5

IT'S a warm and windy day in San Rafael, California.

Ahhh, October 31st. Halloween, baby. Man, can't believe it's so warm here this late into fall. I feel concrete under my bare feet and smell sea water. When I look around I find myself in some alley behind a department store near the dumpsters. Charming. Well, what were they gonna do, have me step through the veil directly onto the middle of Main Street? Big, sexy me just appearing out of thin air as I step from one world to another? Not exactly inconspi... inconspes... Not exactly under the radar.

Still, I have to get out there at some point, but my anxiety is beginning to percolate. I mean, I know it's Halloween, everyone's gonna be dressed up in costumes, and I'll blend right in. But still. I operate in the shadows. I hide behind trees. I don't just walk around in public. But whatever, it's Halloween. This is the one day a year where I can just stroll the streets freely, and I'm gonna make the most of it.

I take out my digital stopwatch to check the BMC clock. Fifty-nine minutes and change to go in the first period. Man, the time difference between Hell and Earth is pretty jarring. My last clash was in 1981. I went back to Hell for only a couple months, now it's already 1983! Hours and hours and hours go by here on Earth before a single hour passes in Hell. So this stopwatch is gonna come in handy.

I take a deep breath and head towards the end of the alley.

Cars drive by up ahead. Pedestrians stroll the sidewalks. Oh, boy. I peek my head out and look around. Here I am, in Norman Rockwell's Anywhere, USA. I look up and there's two of my little hummingbird friends hovering nearby. I guess the other six drones are already following my soon-to-be victims as they prepare for the wonderful night they have planned.

Okay, fuck it. Time to take the plunge. Don't be a baby, Marvin. It's just a leisurely walk down the street... in broad daylight. So I do just that. With two long strides, here I am, standing out on the sidewalk.

I stand there for a second looking around. Not exactly a bustling metropolis, but there are people around and nobody's started screaming yet. Most people aren't in costume as it's still daylight, but there's a few exceptions. A mother walks with her little boy and he's wearing a cheap Frankenstein monster costume. Two more older kids chase each other on the other side of the street, one dressed like a ghost while the other is presumably Superman, though the costume is honestly so bad, I can't really tell.

Holiday decorations line the store fronts. Fake spiderwebs. Plastic skeletons. Multi-colored corn on the cobb. Fake orange leaves; I guess they don't really have a proper Fall in California where the leaves change. Oh, and pumpkins, of course. I smile as I begin to walk, taking it all in. "Monster Mash" plays on a small radio at the entrance to the candy shop. Fucking great song. I hum and snap my fingers. Oh shit, am I strutting?

A young couple with their two young kids are coming the opposite way down the sidewalk. The mother and father visibly tense up when they see me and try not to make eye contact. The mother holds her son's hand more tightly and they both pick up the pace, pushing past and pretending to ignore me. Ha!

I see a newsstand up ahead and slow down to take a look. The proprietor appears to be an aging Indian man dressed in a bad Dracula costume, complete with white face paint and trickles of fake blood coming from the corners of his mouth. He finishes selling a newspaper to a customer when he sees me approach and his demeanor changes. All at once his smile drops, his eyes go wide, and his body tenses. Nothing to see here, friend. Just a fellow citizen in his Halloween costume.

I smile politely and give him a wave.

"Hello," I say casually as I begin to peruse.

"H-hi..." he says.

My eyes quickly scan across the various headlines and front pages of the newspapers and magazines on display. There's some local papers with headlines about some boring new legislation being discussed, then some more about some kind of war going on overseas. The cover of *Time* magazine has a photo of some beat-up Marines carrying a particularly fucked up brother on a gurney, with a headline reading, "Carnage In Beirut - Mideast Madness Hits The Marines." Hm, kooky.

Wait, where the fuck is Beirut? Oh, who cares?

Another headline catches my eye: "The Dead—*LIVE*

tonight in San Rafael!" What? The Dead? Oh I see, it's The Grateful Dead. Bunch of fucking hippies. There's a photo of their leader singing and playing a guitar, and presumably this guy has a name, but to me he looks like Santa's pot-head younger brother. Stoner Claus, that's what I'll call him. In any case, it looks like Stoney and his boys will be playing tonight at the Marin County Amphitheater for a special Halloween show.

Hmmm, I wonder if I'll have time after my clash to go to the concert, maybe slaughter the entire band on stage in front of their adoring fans. Yeah, let's see just how grateful they are! Ah, there probably won't be time, and I wouldn't know how to get to that show anyway... whatever.

I glance back at the newsstand guy and he's still staring. Trembling, as a matter of fact. I give him a great-big, toothy smile. That for some reason only seems to make him even more scared. What the hell, my new teeth look good!

"Like my costume?" I ask, trying to lighten things up.

"Oh, y-yes," he says with a shudder. "V-very scary."

"I'm supposed to be—"

"M-Marvin Brumlow," he blurts out. "The w-worst serial killer in American history. B-body disappeared from the m-morgue. S-some people think he's still... out there... s-somewhere."

Wow, this guy knows his shit. Well, he does work at a news stand. I bet he's read every article about me in every paper and magazine. Really, I'm pretty flattered.

I think I'll murder him.

"Want an autograph?" I ask him, stepping closer.

"N-No, no thank y-you. Really, you don't have t—"

I grab him by the throat before he can scream. Let's see, how should I do it? Neck break? Head pop? Rip his heart out? Maybe something ironic, like kill him with a newspaper somehow? I see his box cutter sitting on top of a stack of newspapers and forget all pretense of trying to be clever. He uses this simple tool to cut off the strings binding the various periodicals and I am certainly not above using it myself.

He gags and sputters, struggling against my grip like a child resisting his father's discipline. Sorry, buddy. Daddy will always have his way. So, I grab that boxcutter, extend the little triangular blade, and slash it across his bulging belly. At first there's just the thin red line, but then it opens up and those glorious intestines come oozing out like a nice, runny egg.

Fake Dracula's eyes bug out and his whole body stiffens up as he feels his hot guts splatting down onto his feet. He reaches a trembling hand like he's calling for help, but the closest person is all the way across the street and not even looking. And besides, I promised him an autograph and damn it, I'm a man of my word.

So I drop the boxcutter to the ground and proceed to shoot my right hand into his gaping wound. His eyes go even wider as he feels me feeling around in there. When I pull my hand out, it's dripping with thick, dark blood. I release my grip of Dracula's throat and let him crash to the pavement, desperately trying to scoop his gizzards back in. I scoop up the latest copy of The Marin Independent Journal and use my dripping finger to sign my name right across the front page.

"Mar-vin," I say as I write my first name in red.

I drop the signed newspaper onto the chest of the dying man. Stupefied, he looks up at me as he rapidly bleeds to death. I smile politely and say "bye" as I continue walking, wiping my bloody hand off on my overalls. Had to get 'em gooey sometime, so fuck it.

I hear screams and commotion.

Someone sees what I did and starts freaking out. Two people on the sidewalk far behind me are pointing and crying. "Look! Look!" someone yells, "Call the police!" Someone else says, "Look, there he goes!" "Look at the size of him!" "Oh my God!" Well shit, what did I expect killing someone on the street in broad daylight?

I see and hear and feel people closing in, and pretty soon this scene will turn into a mob of angry townspeople with pitchforks and torches chasing Boris Karloff into a windmill. Sure, I could go on a rampage and just start killing everyone and anyone in sight, but I'm here to do a job and, Halloween or not, I have to try and stay hidden. So as I start to feel the noose tighten, I duck down another alley, and before anyone can follow me, presto! I step back through the veil. Ha ha!

Now on the other side, I can see them all arrive at the head of the alley, dumbfounded as to where I might have gone. Sorry folks, just call me Batman. I can vanish into thin air at will and I just love it. But enough fooling around. I consult with my notes on the location of this little party I'm supposed to crash and cheerfully head off in that direction.

CHAPTER 6

IT REALLY IS A LOVELY DAY. Well, it's kind of hard to tell when you're behind the veil in the shadow... dimension... thingie. Place. Purgatory, ghost world. It's the same as the physical plane, but cold and gray, and sounds are muffled. It's like I'm looking at the world through frosted glass. But it's either stay behind the veil or just walk the full mile and a half to the target location in plain sight.

I pass a movie theater and check out the marquee.

Looks like they've got *Never Say Never Again* — oh, I guess it's a new Bond movie, cool — *The Big Chill, All The Right Moves, Deathstalker* — might have to check that one out — and *The Dead Zone*. Hmm, I like the sound of that. Dead Zone. That's where I am right now, this place in between worlds, behind the veil, where lost souls wander. That's a good name for it... I'm stealing it.

I keep walking through the dead zone, following the directions in my notes. Heading away from downtown and into a residential area. A very nice one, too, if I might add. I see some big houses, or I should say mansions. Beamers and Rolls Royces drive past. A few very young children in costumes are already out trick-or-treating with their parents. Palm trees and ocean breeze. I could get used to this.

I turn up West Seaview Avenue and this little one-lane road is taking me up into the hills. Steep hills. Pretty soon I'm sweatin' and huffin' and need a rest. Shit. *Hoo!* man, this is a steep fucking hill. I'm already winded. So I stand here for a minute with my hands on my hips like a little bitch and catch my breath.

Deciding to pace myself and take my time, I proceed.

The winding seaside road goes up and up, and houses become few and farther between. Each is a little castle, a grand display of opulence. And each is lined with trees on all sides. Rich people like their privacy. I love it. Finally, I reach the top of the hill and there's only one house up here by itself, surrounded by trees and over-looking the San Francisco Bay and the Golden Gate Bridge.

Yup, 40 West Seaview Ave, this is the place. Nice.

It's a two-story mesa style house, stucco walls, red terracotta shingles on the roof. A motorized iron front gate. There's a donut-shaped driveway with a little foun-tain in the center, trickling water and surrounded by small cactuses. Cacti. Whatever.

I hear music and it's not *completely* terrible, so I step through the veil into the real world and move in a little closer. In the center of the driveway is a silver Jaguar sportster, dripping wet and covered with soap suds. And there's the first of my next flock of sheep. Working a big, soapy sponge over the surface of the car and singing along badly to the music, it's none other than Richard. Little white shorts. Pink polo shirt. Ugh, fucking gag me. But the song he's listening to has a nice swingin' 50's vibe, and the singer is talking about being a cool cat, hanging out in alleys, but being above having to chase little mice around. I can dig that.

In any case, I've made a note to myself to make Richard's demise extra special. I don't have anything planned yet per se, but it has to be particularly painful, especially brutal. So I'll just keep my eyes open and improvise. Meantime, while frat boy is polishing his surrogate cock, I check my stopwatch to see where I'm at.

Only twenty minutes has gone by on the Hell clock. Crazy, I've already been in here for two or three hours. I look around but I don't see any of the other kids yet. There's only three hummingbird drones floating around me right now which means the other five are following the rest of the soon-to-be victims. Wonder what they're doing...I contemplate just taking Richard out right now, as he's here alone, a perfect sitting duck. But it's still early and I haven't come up with a brilliant enough demise for him yet, so I'll hold off.

That turns out to be a good call, as I hear a pair of engines coming up the street. Two cars pull up to the gate and I hunch down into the bushes to hide. The drivers both start beeping their horns and Richard chuckles, taking out his clicker and letting them in. The iron gate rolls open and the first vehicle I see pull in is a green-and-white Dodge van. Behind it is an eggshell VW Bug with patches of bare primer showing through. Wait a second... a VW Bug? Again? I know one of the kids had a Bug last time and I'm pretty sure there was one in my first clash, too. Right?

So weird. What are the chances? And what does it mean?

While I squat amongst the hydrangeas, the gracious host greets his guests as they pull up and park behind his Jag. Jumping out of the driver's seat of the van is Noelle, looking light and springy and super cute in her *Alice in Wonderland* costume. Stephanie hops out of the passenger door looking like Farrah Fawcett showing up to a red carpet event, complete with a mink stole, and Parker gets out of the back sliding door, wearing a piss-poor excuse for a pirate costume. Seriously, an eye patch, bandana, pencilled-on mustache and goatee, skull and crossbones painted on his t-shirt. And oh yeah, a cheap plastic sword. Ugh.

"Hey, hot stuff!" Richard says, embracing Noelle and kissing her.

"Where's your costume?" she asks.

"I'll put it on later."

The VW's engine cuts and Kareem steps out from the driver's seat. Jeans, t-shirt, Adidas, letterman jacket... Guess he's too cool to wear a costume. Yeah, big man smiles with his perfect pearly whites, his jheri-curl glistening impeccably. Mo stumbles out front the passenger door, nearly twisting her ankle on a six-inch high heel and cursing under her breath. She finally rights herself and straightens out her hot-pink tube skirt. Long pink nails, pink-framed sunglasses, bling everywhere. I guess this is a Halloween costume?

She shuffles around to the front of the car, a bright-red wig of curly fries bouncing on her head as she moves. Kareem gives her a quick kiss and helps himself to a handful of ass. Ahhh, gotta love it. I watch as the two lovebirds meet up with the rest of the group, exchanging smiles and high fives.

"Shit, you give me a hard time about not having *my* costume?" Richard jokes. "What are *you* wearing, Kareem?"

"Pssh, I'm too cool to wear a costume."

See! What'd I say?

"And *I'm* fabulous," Mo says, pouting her lips and striking a pose. Everyone laughs. Don't know why, it wasn't funny. Whatever.

"What time does the party start?" Parker asks.

"Seven," Richard says. "We don't have to leave for two hours. Everyone relax."

"We're coming back here after, right?" Stephanie asks.

"Yes, sweetie," Noelle says, "Don't worry, you have a place to crash."

Hm, leaving for a party in two hours. Should I allow that? Maybe I should just disable their cars now to make sure they can't leave. Then again, it's been a while since I went to a party. Why not? I'll just go to the party, walk around in plain sight, dance with some babes, throw back a few brews, then come back here to the house and take care of business! Still, where is this party and how would I get there? Also, that would mean letting a lot of time go by without giving the fans back home a good kill.

Then again, just killing them all here in the house in the next couple hours would be kind of anticlimactic. Hm... I'll think about it, play it by ear.

In any case, I see my new friends are starting to head inside, so I'd better move and follow them to see better.

One by one they walk through the front door. I see Parker kick the ground like a child and say, "I still say we should go to The Dead show instead..."

Sorry, buddy. You ain't going to see The Dead tonight. You gonna *be* dead, and lemme tell you, you ain't gonna be very grateful about it.

CHAPTER 7

I CROSS AROUND to the backyard to find a better spot to watch from. Three of my little hummingbird-fucker buddies buzz around me while the other four are inside following the kids. Can't see or hear them right now so I need to find a good window I can park myself at. Also, it doesn't help that somewhere close by, somebody is mowing their lawn or blowing leaves or something. Ugh. I hate that.

When I get to the back I'm greeted by a huge wall of windows spanning nearly the entire rear of the house, but what really catches my eye is the pool. It's big and blue, with some nice patio furniture placed around and a covered jacuzzi at the other end of the yard. Nice. Man, fuck these kids, can't I just take a swim and sit in the jacuzzi for a while? Go inside, just kill everyone super quick, plop down and watch some football on their big screen, get nice and drunk...

Nah, doesn't make for compelling television.

I can't walk out into the open back here because the whole yard is visible through that huge wall of windows. I could slip into the dead zone but I'd rather not use that as a crutch if I don't have to. But I can hear their muffled voices inside and see the slightest hint of their shadows and reflections from my angle near the edge of the windows. Gotta find a better vantage point.

There was nothing on the left side of the house, where I crossed before, so I head back around the front and try the right side of the house. There's a couple windows, one peeking in on a bedroom, and one a bathroom. I reach a side door with a flimsy-looking lock (nice), and just beyond it is another window. I take a look in and can see quite clearly into the kitchen. And there they all are.

My new group of six has convened around the kitchen table, or that thing in the middle of the floor, the uh... island. Beers have been cracked open and the little group of "friends" seems to be having a lovely time. Still, I can barely hear anything they're saying. The fucking noise of lawnmowers and leaf-blowers is even louder now on this side of the house. Come on, man! Shut the fuck up! Fucking bastards must be landscaping one of the houses next door. Somebody needs to go over there and tell those assholes to shut the fu...

Hey. Wait a second. I'll just go murder them!

My new flock of sheep ain't going nowhere for a little bit. I have time. And I know the fans are getting antsy for blood and guts. Never let it be said that Marvin Brumlow doesn't give the fans what they want. So I take a quick look around and it doesn't take long to find the source of the fucking noise pollution.

Sure enough, it's coming from the house right behind me. There are trees and hedges in between homes, so I spread open the leaves a little bit and poke my head in to see the back yard of the neighbor's house. And there they are, three of them, one trimming hedges, the other two blowing leaves.

I'm going to call them Juan, Hector, and Carlos. No no, not Carlos. That's too predictable. I'm mixing things up this time, subverting expectations. Challenging the norm and questioning everything. So no, I don't think his name is Carlos. I think it's... Glenn. No, Leroy! There we go. Leroy Hernandez, Venezuelan landscaper! Hey, why not? It could happen. His mama got preggers back in Guatemala, got dumped by the daddy and came here to the U.S. where she met Bobby Ray, a brotha' from San Fran who thinks the baby is his... I don't know how it happened and I don't care.

His name is Leroy. Shut up.

I watch as Juan, Hector, and Leroy continue with their obnoxious work, unaware of me lurking behind the property divide. Juan and Hector look about middle-age, each with a substantial cerveza-gut, each operating a wailing leaf blower. Guys, it's Cali, how many leaves can there *be* on the ground? You never heard of a rake? Yes, judgment has been passed, you deserve to die. Leroy is the youngest, fit and healthy, and trimming the bushes with a pretty badass hedge trimmer.

This will be fun. I squeeze between two whatever-the-fuck-they-are kind of trees and press up against the wall between properties, which comes only halfway up my chest. I easily hop and push myself up, landing on top of the wall like fucking Spider-Man. I make sure to strike a pose as I see the drone cameras filming me in the corner of my eye. I hop down onto the other side.

I crouch down low and sneak along the inside of the wall, staying behind a row of bushes. These guys are just blowing random little leaves around and chatting it up, oblivious. Man, los muchachos are really small too! Like, as I get closer I can tell they only come up to my waist. I'm seven fucking feet tall, so *everyone* is short next to me, but dude, these boys are fucking Oompa Loompas!

Okay, so I'll use that as a humorous and ironic twist to their deaths. They're short, so I'll make them even shorter! Juan and Hector are working together and standing close, so I'll take them out at once, quickly and quietly before they can scream. My plan is to literally squash them vertically down into the ground so they won't be five-foot two, they'll be six inches tall and just a mess of bones and skin and guts.

So I creep closer, closer, wait for it... wait for it...

Now! I jump out of my hiding place, hands high over my head, and land in between my unsuspecting friends. As I come down, I strike down with both hands, aiming to swat each of them on the top of the head and smash them into pulp as I land in one fell swoop. Well, it kinda half goes that way.

My left hand hits Hector square on top of the head and I successfully follow through and crush him down into the ground like an empty beer can. His skull and spine crush and shatter as they are forced down through his clavicle, then collapse through the ribcage, fucking devastating all internal organs and tissues, ripping through the hips, legs shattering, blood erupting every-where... Hector looks like a crushed bug on the windshield.

My right hand, however, misses Juanito's cabesa.

I guess he heard me coming from behind and turned, because now he's ducking out of the way as my hand swipes down. Juan gasps in horror as this horrible, monstrous giant — Me! — towers over him and brutally squashes his amigo right in front of him. He backs up, still holding the leaf blower but now wielding it as if to fend me off. Dios mío. That's not gonna stop me, buddy. In fact, I want to thank you for offering me such a lovely murder weapon to use on you.

I grab him by the throat before he can scream and snatch that fucking noise maker out of his hand. A big tube connected to a backpack, a machine for blowing air. Okay then, my ironic twist on this one will be that I jam the fucking end of the hose into his mouth, then blast it on high and fill him up with hot air. I envision him being filled up so much that he literally explodes after too much pressure has built up, bloody chunks of him just flying everywhere...

Oh yeah, this'll be a good one. I grab the end of the hose, position it in front of his mouth, and start to press. But it's not going the way I envisioned in my head. The nozzle — end of the hose, whatever it's called — is just too big to fit into his mouth. That, plus he's squirming and fighting and it's worse than trying to feed a toddler. I notice that I'm shattering his front teeth, he's screaming, there's a little blood dribbling, so that's all good, but... I don't know.

I want that great visual of sticking the hose all the way down his throat and blowing him up! Guess that's not entirely realistic. I could maybe rip his jaw off, then force the hose down his throat, but it's all just feeling really awkward, and I realize that what I'd envisioned isn't very practical. Still, I have to fucking do something.

Before I can make a decision, it's made for me. Oh, Leroy.

Like a young hero, he comes to save his amigo, waving the long, serrated blades of the hedge trimmer and screaming at me in a rage. He lunges forward, trying to slash me, and it's pretty intimidating, I must say. I don't want to get cut by that thing—that would hurt! It's like a long, skinny chainsaw! Sure, if he kills me I'd just come back, but still, it fucking sucks. So I dodge the attack, still holding Juan by the throat with one hand.

I feel the best way to dispatch Juan right now is to let his friend do it for me, so as I see Leroy about to lunge forward with that fucking gas-powered sword, I thrust Juan forward directly into the direction of the blade and... presto! The rotating blade of the hedge trimmer shreds through poor Juanito's chest, and begins to sputter and smoke as the small motor strains.

Leroy's eyes light up in shock and horror as he disembowels his friend. Or just his co-worker... I don't know if they're friends or not, fuck off. But there they are, face to face, as the motor continues to spin those blades, blending up Juan's guts like we're making a margarita until Leroy finally lets go of the trigger.

The hedge trimmer stops sputtering and Leroy lets go. Juan staggers back, the giant turkey carver spearing through his torso, blood gushing and sloshing out of him, and finally falls down dead. Leroy cries and mumbles something in Mexican, starts to hyperventilate, looks like he's building up to one big, unbridled, scream-at-the-top-of-your-lungs type of scream. Well, obviously I don't want to make too much noise and alert my new friends next door, so I can't let him do that.

I have no weapon in hand and no brilliant ideas are springing to mind. Head squash? Head squash. I wrap my hand around the top of his head, give it a good, quick squeeze and, *pop*. Ahhh, never gets old. I know I've done it before and it's not the most original thing, but it's just so much *fun*. I mean, the eyeballs squirt out from between my fingers, skull bones instantly crunch and pop, blood and brains and goo just fucking spraying everywhere, feels all warm and goopey... I mean, what's not to love?

Leroy's body falls to the ground, blood spraying from the stump where his head was into the soil. His whole body tenses with a violent twitch, then finally goes limp. Nice. I kneel down and wipe my bloody hand off on Leroy's clothes.

Adios, amigos.

All in all, I think that went well. A couple things didn't go my way and I had to improvise, but I got the job done. See folks, unlike our pal Larry "The Snapper," I actually face adversity and have to overcome it. I don't just have magical powers where I can do whatever I want. I'm the *people's* champion, baby. And I'm coming for my belt, motherfuckers!

CHAPTER 8

I CROSS BACK to the other house where my targets are partying and sneak up to the south wall. Gotta take a piss. No hummingbird fuckers buzzing around and watching me, so fuck it. I whip it out and hose that shit down. Ahhhhh, nice and foamy... Now, where was I? Oh yeah, got some kids to kill.

I can hear their muffled voices from inside already. Maybe I'll try to get in to hear better, go into the dead zone and watch them like a ghost. Actually, before I do that, I remember to check my game clock, and sure enough, there's only two minutes and fifteen seconds until first period ends.

Ha! See, now I know not to go in there right now because I'm expecting to get yanked right out and back into the Grand Malavista Arena. So instead, I circle around the house, find a window I can see them through, and bide my time. Looks like Richard and Noelle are in the kitchen while the other four are drinking brewskis in the living room. Mmm, Pabst Blue Ribbon. Good choice.

Then I feel that familiar grip from the other side.

I'm suddenly pulled back through the veil.

BACK IN HELL, BABY.

Lights flash and the crowd roars. I hold my hands up

and wave to everyone as I stand center stage in the spot-light. Oh, the looks on everyone's faces! They adore me! Well, Snapper doesn't seem to like me much, and I see him over there talking into his microphone, doing his little commentary. Go ahead and talk that shit, pussy.

Jim and my corner-men run up to greet me with towels and a bottle of water. I drink deeply while Turi hands me a nice, plush towel. Jim smiles and gives me a big thumbs-up, smackin' away on that fucking gum, as always.

"Really, really nice, man," he says. "Loved that full body squash! These people fuckin' ate it up, man!"

"Yeah, you're killin' it, Marv!" Turi says.

"You really think so?" I ask.

"Totally, man," Jim says in between gum smacks. "Everyone can't wait to see what you come up with next. Me included! How you feeling?"

"Fine."

"Ready to kick it into high gear?"

Ten seconds left on the clock.

I look over at Larry. We make eye contact.

"Oh yeah," I grumble. "Let's fuckin' do this."

BACK IN THE LAND OF THE LIVING.

I'm here in the same spot I was standing before the break, looking into the kitchen and living room of the house through a side window. There's Kareem and Mo sitting in the love seat, while Parker and Stephanie couldn't be farther apart. They're all hanging out in the living room and once again I have to wonder, why are these people friends? Hell, *nobody* wants to be around Parker, and he doesn't seem to notice despite their not-at-all-subtle body language that screams *fuck off, dude.*

Richard and Noelle are nowhere in sight. Hmmm. I cross around, looking in through windows and putting my ear against the wall. Then I hear them. In the bedroom. Hee hee. Sounds like they're just talking right now, but I can already tell what loverboy is doing. He's trying to get himself a little slice of cake before the party, of course. Naturally, I want to watch.

I'm gonna have to go inside the house now, which means I need to use the dead zone. I open up the veil and step through it, and now here I am. It's cold, it's gray, it sucks being here, but I can be right in the room with someone and be a complete ghost to them. So yeah, it's my best friend.

Now that I'm invisible, I casually walk around the house, testing doors and windows. The sliding patio doors are unlocked but the kids are inside not too far away. I wonder if they'll notice the door sliding open on its own. Fuck it. Gently, slowly, I slide that fucker open. It's pretty smooth and quiet and no one seems to notice. Not bad. So I duck my head to get through the door and step inside.

My foot touches down on old, wood floors, and the boards fart out a loud creak. Shit. I step the rest of the way inside, trying to minimize the squeaking of the old floor boards. Good luck with that, I'm four hundred fucking pounds. That shit squeaks loud. Stephanie notices.

"What was that?" she asks, getting up from her seat.

"What?" Parker says with a dumb look on his dumb face.

"Sounded like someone's walking around back there. Hello?"

Stephanie comes over here to look around, walking right by me. Mmmm, sweet little girl. She notices the open sliding door and goes over to it.

"Did we leave this open?" she asks, concerned.

"Looks that way," Kareem says with a smirk, more focused on Mo's cleavage than anything else. Get it while you can, buddy.

Stephanie rubs her shoulders and slides the door shut, locking it.

Parker tries to soothe her nerves by offering her a drink but she declines, as expected. While they squabble, I sneak away. I want to see what's going on with Richard and Noelle. Up on my tip-toes I creep through the hallways until I find the door, and I hear them in there. Shit, I need to see what's happening.

Suddenly, the door flies open and Noelle storms out.

I jump out of the way as Richard chases her. Miss Thing is straightening up her Alice In Wonderland costume, her eyes all puffy and her lips all pouty. Awww.

"Babe, what's the problem?" Richard demands, grabbing her arm.

"I'm sorry, Richard. I'm just not ready."

Yeah, *Richard.* You need to respect her boundaries.

"B-but I thought you were... I thought we were... y'know!"

"I'm sorry," she says, leaning against the banister in the hallway. "I just... I have a lot to process in my mind.

Guess I haven't fully healed from that night yet. Don't know if I ever will."

What night?

"Look babe," Richard says, stepping in and rubbing her shoulders, "we've been going together for a year now. There's only so many cold showers I can take."

"I know, it's just... be patient with me, okay?"

He sighs, "Okay."

They kiss. Little pitiful peck on the lips.

"C'mon," Noelle says, "we should get back to the others."

Richard sheepishly agrees and allows her to lead him down the stairs. I can practically hear the air fizzling out of his boner like a busted ballon. Poor guy. And shit, once again, an ambiguous relationship! So weird, but what does it mean?

Back to the living room and here's all six of our contestants back together. Looks like they're discussing the plan for the night, which is good for me. I like to know what they're doing, where they're going, what they're expecting to happen and when. Helps me plan and execute their... well, their executions, more effectively.

"Look," Kareem says, stroking Mo's shoulders and never breaking eye contact with her, "I got everything I need right here. Why don't we all just chill here?"

"Dude, come on! This party is going to be totally rad!" Parker says.

"Yeah," Stephanie adds, "I want to see if there's any hot guys there."

I make sure to check Parker's reaction as she says this and watch him deflate as his soul dies just a little bit. It's a thing of beauty. And really, Parker, do you *really* expect a fucking dime like Stephanie to be into you? And Richard is responsible for playing matchmaker with these two? Why would he ever think she would go for him? I have questions!

"Guys, we don't have to stay there all night," Noelle says. "Why don't we just go for a while and have some fun, then come back here later?"

"Yeah, baby," Mo says, "I want to dance! Wanna get my drank on!"

Kareem sighs. "Okay, fine. So, we all takin' the van then?"

"Nah man, I'm already a little buzzed," Richard says. "Let's just walk. It's only two miles and it's a warm night."

"Yeah!" Stephanie adds with enthusiasm. "We can see all the little trick-or-treaters running around!"

Good plan. That way I can follow you.

I had considered taking care of them all here. Disable their cars, cut the phone lines, the usual. But hell, why not have a little fun with this one? How long has it been since I've been to a proper party? A party where everyone is wearing makeup and costumes and I'll blend right in? Yes, let's all go to the party. Marvin wants to dance!

CHAPTER 9

TRA-LA-LA-LA-LAAAA, walking down the street with my new buddies.

This is nice. Richard, Noelle, Stephanie, Parker, Kareem and Mo are strolling their way to this Halloween party and I'm right behind them in the dead zone. While they chat and laugh and talk about stupid shit, I'm swinging my arms, drumming on my thighs, hell, I even catch myself skipping for a minute. Just feels nice to be out walking around, even if I am behind the veil where everything is cloudy and gray.

As promised, Richard has changed into his costume, which is just his recycled tux from prom, yet he says he's going as James Bond. Fair enough. At least he's putting in more effort than Kareem. That's okay, buddy, I have something special in mind for you. If I time it right and the stars align and I can make it work, oh, it will be just delightful.

But what about the others? I think I've figured out what I want to do with Parker and Noelle, but that can always change with circumstances. Not sure what to do with Stephanie and Mo yet, and I'm drawing a blank on Richard. I've made a note to make his death especially grisly and agonizing, but coming up with something truly original is no easy feat. Everything's been done!

I listen to them chit-chat as we move from the hills of

the upscale neighborhood to a stretch near the coast. I smell the sea water, hear the waves crashing... ahhhh, this is nice. To the left I start to see these really cool little inlets and tributaries. Cute, mossy marshes with old, small docks and fishing boats, ramshackle sheds, bunch of burly dudes bringing in their catch... this is my kind of place!

Makes me want to go fishing. As I've said many times before, if my daddy ever taught me anything besides being horrible and cruel and murderous, it was fishing. Shit, I could probably find some good fishing spots when I get back to Hell. Would have to go outside the city, of course. Probably need a fishing license, get a pole, tackle-box, some lures, baits, nice vest... one of those hats with the netting... folding chair... bring some beers...

Wait, where was I? Oh right, shit. Following these kids.

I can think about fishing later. Right now, it looks like Parker is slowing down and holding up the group, so naturally I stop to see what's up, too. Fat Boy Pirate is gawking at something across the way, nearly drooling.

"You guys! Look!" Parker shouts, pointing his finger.

It's the Marin County Veteran's Auditorium. Amphitheater. Whatever.

"Yeah, so?" Richard asks.

"Duuuude! The Dead are playing there tonight! *The Grateful Dead!*"

"Pssh. Nah man, fuck that shit," Kareem says.

"Aw, come on, you guys!"

They begin to squabble and bitch about it, and I get it. Your favorite band is playing so close, yet your friends are a bunch of dipshits and won't let you go. The place is close but not *right* across the street. I could throw a football and hit it, it's so close. But I'm super fucking strong, so I can throw a football a lot farther than normal. Obviously. Anyway, the gang pries poor Parker away and he mopes along behind them.

"I wanna partyyyy!" Mo shouts, hooting and dancing as she struts.

She is so annoying. I'm so happy it's my job to murder her in the most creatively brutal fashion I can think of. I'm thinking it's gonna have to be something involving the wig. I mean, that wig is just ridiculous. Maybe I can set the wig on fire or something, let those synthetic fibers melt down into her brain. We'll see.

"Relax, we're almost there," Richard says.

I see a pedestrian who doesn't look like the others, and it takes me a second to realize that it's a ghost! I almost forgot that behind the veil, in the dead zone, it's purgatory. This is where lost souls go, so yeah, from time to time, I'm going to see a ghost in here. This one looks like a businessman, carrying a briefcase, wearing a hat. His style is straight out of the fifties. This guy must have died while walking around on these streets and is now just in limbo. Maybe he had a massive coronary, or got hit by a bus? Either way, there he is just going about his business like nothing happened.

We share a look and he seems to be a bit taken aback by my appearance. Yes, even lost souls in purgatory find me horrifying. Good. I give him a little wave and keep walking. Makes me wonder how Hank and all my charbroiled buddies are doing back at the Chapman Institute...

So, we get to the party.

It's at a bar/nightclub/whatever. I hear the music blasting from the street. People stand in line to get in, wearing their Halloween best. I see a witch, a Dracula, a Superman, and a naughty nurse, of course. There's some pretty cool costumes here, I have to say, and we haven't even gotten inside yet. One guy has fabricated a whole robot suit for himself out of foil and aluminum sheeting, complete with blinking lights. One chick is Vampirella or something, but nobody told her she don't have the titties to fill out the costume, so it's kind of underwhelming.

My six young friends get right in line.

Well, I'm not waiting around. And I don't need to pay at the door; I can just go in while I'm in the dead zone, then slip out any time I want. I start to head for the door when I suddenly stop. A thought hits me.

It's been a little while since I killed someone.

Now, I'm planning to go inside, hang out while these idiots party, then follow them home again... Too much time without any deaths. I should probably try to get in a quick kill before I go inside, so I look around.

A block down the street I see a guy alone in a phone booth.

Perfect. I walk across the street and head towards my target. He's in a shady area away from all the foot traffic, and as I get closer, I see he's dressed as a clown. Puffy clothes, makeup, red nose and pink wig, this guy put in some effort on this. Nice, I've always wanted to kill a clown. Now it looks like he's trying to coax his girlfriend over the phone to meet him at the party and not having much luck.

I have a window of about fifteen seconds to act before other pedestrians come into range, so I quickly step out from behind the veil and into the "real world." I pick up the pace, clenching my fists.

I stomp up to the door of the phone booth and push it open. Bozo turns, and I can't see his face because I'm taller than the door of the booth, but I imagine he's looking out at my chest and seeing nothing but a pair of bloody overalls and hairy shoulders. I shoot my hand in, fish around for his head, and grab it.

He shrieks. I yank him forward and force his face through one of the square window panes in the door, shattering the glass. He sputters and gags, shards embedded in his face, leaking blood everywhere. I smash his head down, aiming his throat for the broken glass at the bottom of the frame. It slices through his larynx, carotid artery and esophagus, and all it takes is a few little pushes down to break the spine and pop that sucker right off.

Bing, there you go. Just like opening a Coke bottle.

The clown's head falls to the outside while his body collapses, the arterial spray from his neck stump really shooting up high, painting the entire interior of the phone booth red. It's really pretty impressive and cool to see. I notice a pair of 3D glasses sticking out of his pocket, so grab them. Love these things. But I can't wait around, so I turn and book it out of there, hoping nobody saw me.

As I walk away, I'm just waiting for some woman to shriek, or some dude to scream "stop that man!" But it doesn't come. Nobody heard that? Weird. In any case, my little flying buddies caught the whole thing, and I know the fans back home enjoyed that one. There you go, you sick bastards, a little something to tide you over.

I hear that pumping disco shit music as I near the club.

I put on my new 3D glasses. Oh yeah, baby. It's party time.

CHAPTER 10

BACK IN THE DEAD ZONE, I approach the front door of the disco, looks like its called *Club Pompino*. Hm, sounds fancy. Well, I'm a ghost right now, so I walk right through the door, through the bodies of the people coming inside. Imagine telling these people that in an alternate dimension, deranged serial killer superstar Marvin Brumlow is occupying the same space as them and basically walking through their bodies! Well, here I am, bitches.

The party is in full swing. Beautiful young people having the time of their lives, just dancing, dancing, dancing. The song is some more of that techno bullshit, but I have to admit it does sound kind of cool. It's a slower tempo song, chick singer, kind of spooky, actually. Could be cool for a future walk-out song, who knows. I can't hear all the lyrics but it sounds like she's singing something about sweet dreams. Cool. I can dig it, baby. I'm hip.

My six friends haven't made it inside yet, so I take some time to stroll around and check out the costumes. Maybe have a drink. Shit, it's a party! But first things first, I have to get out of the dead zone so I can really *be* in the room. I want to be seen. I want to feel like I blend in and have a good time. So what I need to do is find a place where I can step out into the Earthly plane and be inconsp... incons... be sneaky about it. Don't want to just spring into existence right in the middle of the dance floor!

So I find a dark corner where nobody can see, open up the veil, step through with one foot, then slip the rest of my body through. I close the veil up and now here I am. In the real world, baby. But shit, now I'm scared! I mean, am I really about to just stroll into the crowd and see what happens?

Fortune favors the bold, Marvin.

Fuck it.

I step out of the corner and start easing myself into the masses of dancing bodies and flashing lights. Better start bobbing my head to the beat. Yes, that's right everyone, nothing to see here! Pretty cool costume, right? I do my own makeup. Oh, thank you very much, you're so kind. Yeah, I know, I'm really tall. I play basketball. I'm totally *not* a real-life, undead, superhuman mass murderer. Marvin Brumlow? Oh, everyone says that! Haha, I know, right? Thank you so much.

I see a woman in really good witch makeup walk by. Another guy dancing is in a full gorilla suit. One dude is a psycho surgeon, wearing scrubs and a doctor's mask, dripping with fake blood. Another chick is some kind of fairy, Tinkerbell or something. She has some cool shimmery wings and a bangin' little figure. I'm rubbing shoulders with these people and so far getting away with it. Well, their shoulders are rubbing into my forearms, but that's the basic idea.

I am definitely starting to get some looks now, and so far it's pretty amusing. Eyes are going wide, and I can only guess by the expressions on their faces what each must be thinking. Most give a basic *holy shit* wide-eyed stare. But I'm bobbin' my head and trying to move my feet. That's right everyone, just a big guy in a mask, just one of you!

That song I was enjoying ends and a DJ dressed as a tiger wearing sunglasses switches over to a new song. The voice sounds familiar but I can't quite place it. He's telling his opponent to "Beat It" and the party-goers are losing their minds for it. Have to say, this one's kind of not terrible either. Some nice gi-tar work in there, too.

I decide I need a drink.

I go to the bar. The bartender sees me. He freezes.

"Uh, h-hi? Y-yes? U-um..." this guy can't even talk.

"Whiskey," I say.

He reaches a trembling hand and starts to pour a glass, when I stop him, grabbing the bottle and glass from his hand. He gasps and trembles as I step away from the bar. I saunter out closer to the main hub of the party, pouring a full glass of fire water. I down that shit in one gulp. Then another.

Ohhhh yeah, now I'm feeling a little more loose.

I can't help but start to swing my hips. My shoulders begin to move. I'm tapping my feet and moving to the beat, bottle in one hand, glass in the other. Feeling good, feeling alive. Look at me now, fans! You wanna see Marvin cut loose? Okay, here we go!

Now, in case it hasn't been made clear, I do not in fact have any formal dance training. Or any informal dance training. Not sure if I can even remember dancing with other people before. Ever. But that doesn't stop me.

I'm a dynamo out here, baby! I'm spinning, bouncing, moving my hands, kicking my feet. I'm not sure if anything I'm doing would be classified as actual dance moves, but it's all about the attitude.

I'm kinda-sorta moving to the beat, and I haven't tripped and fallen yet, so I see this as a massive success. Other people in the crowd seem to agree, as everyone's eyes have gone wide and they're all giving me space. I've seen movies and TV; people at dance parties do this when one person really shines, so they give him some space, let him have the spotlight, so to speak. The hummingbird fuckers are all here, hovering over the crowd and taking in the whole scene.

That's right, BMC fans back home! Marvin can dance!

I begin to pour another glass of whiskey as I bounce and boogie, but it's spilling everywhere. Fuck it, what do I need a glass for anyway? I lift that bottle up over my head and just pour the rest of the whiskey right into my open mouth. My 3D glasses fall off my face and I don't care.

"Woooo!" I shout, tossing the empty bottle and glass into the crowd.

I hear a faint gasp of alarm and assume the bottle hit somebody. Hahaaa.

I spin round and round. I do a little Irish jig. I jump up and down. I... I don't feel so good. Head's spinning, out of breath, feel that little stitch in my side that always lets me know I'm out of shape. Hoooo, okay. I need to rest.

Over to my right and just past the dance floor is a little area set up with tables and chairs. As I head in that direction, I notice my six friends finally making it through the front door. Shit, I'm over here getting drunk and dancing, making an ass out of myself, and took my eye off the ball. Idiot. Go sit down, Marvin. Sit down, stay out of sight and keep your eyes on the targets, damn it.

The first two to come through the doors are Kareem and Mo, followed by Stephanie, already dancing with her hands high over her head, then Parker, eyes glued to Stephanie's ass, then Richard and Noelle, arm in arm. I find a chair with a good view of the whole room and plop down to watch them better. I'm sweating like a pig and panting for breath. But now I can just compose myself, enjoy the show, and plot my next move. Ideally, I'd like to kill someone soon.

"Hey, man!" Some jerkoff kid dressed as some kind of blue alien, complete with intricate Star Trek-geek-level detail, comes up and playfully swats my shoulder. "Dude, great costume, man!" he shouts in order to be heard over the music. "Marvin Brumlow, right?"

"Umm," I clear my throat, "uh, yeah."

"Awesome, dude! Is that foam rubber, or did you build it all up with liquid latex, cotton and nose-putty, that kind of thing?"

Oh great, a special FX nerd.

"Uh... it's the rubber one."

"Really nice, man! Did you sculpt it yourself?"

"Uh, yeah."

"Really impressive work, dude! You got the whole thing down all the way to the wardrobe! Got the blood spatter and grime looking just *perfect*, man! And you're a really big guy, so you're perfect for a Marvin costume!"

He smiles, admiring me up and down, and honestly, it's starting to creep me the fuck out.

But I see those little hummingbird fuckers hovering, and I know people are watching, so I have to perform. Can't just freeze up and not have any charisma.

"I like your outfit too!" I say with a smile, needing to shout to be heard. "Really nice makeup! I like all the blue colors and that, that headpiece thing is uh, really groovy! Uh, dude!"

"Hahaaa!" he says and slaps my shoulder again. Okay, yeah, now he has to die. "Thanks, buddy! Yeah, I work in FX myself! Me and some of my buddies work over at ILM! It's right here in town! You got talent, dude! We're always looking for guys like you!"

Aha, I see. His little company, whatever it is, they're always looking for guys like me. But I think *he* is always looking for guys like me too. I think my blue alien friend has some ulterior motives here. Okay, I think I know what I need to do.

"What?" I ask, leaning in. "I can't hear you!"

He leans in closer and shouts, "We're always looking for guys like you!"

I act frustrated, shaking my head. "I still can't hear you!" I look around and say, "Can we go somewhere else to talk?"

"Oh, yeah! Yeah, sure!" he says, nearly licking his lips.

I get up and start leading him to the bathroom. He looks me up and down, astonished by my size now that he actually sees me standing.

"My God! You really *are* huge!" he shouts.

"In here!" I say, pointing to the bathroom. "Maybe we can find some privacy!"

I do my best to flirt with this little tulip, and I can see he's anticipating a hot, impromptu hookup session in the John. Good. Keep thinking that. I'll be your big, hot beefcake tonight, baby.

We come into the bathroom and there are a couple other guys in here, but at least it's a little quieter. One dude is just finishing up and washing his hands, and he's out of there pretty quick. I wash my hands to bide my time while we wait for the last guy to leave the bathroom.

Meanwhile, my little alien buddy is eyeing me up and down, continuing to compliment my "costume." Keep talking, buddy. I watch as the last guy flushes and leaves without washing his hands - gross. Finally it's just the two of us together and he's eyeing me like a hungry dog.

"Why don't we go into the stall?" I say. "More private."

"Yeah," he says, "oh, yeah..."

So, I duck my head and go into the stall, and my "date" is right behind me. He slams the door shut once we're both inside and latches it tight. He turns to me. His eyes are full of desire. He hurls himself at me, trying to touch, trying to kiss.

Nope.

Instead, I pivot and grab him by the back of the head, then shove his face down into the toilet. Pissy water splashes all over the me as I muscle his face deeper down. He flails and spasms and struggles, but let's face it, I'm forcing his skull through a hole the size of a tennis ball. This doesn't take long.

Bone crunches and the ceramic shit-bowl cracks as I squash his entire head into the hole, right down to the neck. The toilet begins to bubble and foam, with blood and water leaking out. Oh, shit. I better get out of here before the fucking place floods. Better get back to my six little piggies. I think it may be time to introduce myself.

CHAPTER 11

FIRST THING'S FIRST, before I leave this bathroom stall and head back into the club, I'm slipping into the dead zone. Time to stop being so stupid. Dancing around, drinking, calling attention to myself. Come on, Marvin. You had your fun, now it's time to get serious. I can maybe blend in for a little while, but how long until somebody notices that I'm not wearing makeup and this is no costume? How long until someone comes into the bathroom and sees the mess I've made?

Yup, time to go.

Now behind the cover of the veil, I walk back out into the club as a ghost. It's cold, gray, the music is muffled, and everything looks like I'm seeing it through funky-old glass, but I'm able to go unseen again. Much more comfortable. I'm also pretty much drunk as a skunk after downing nearly a whole bottle of Jack, so being in the dead zone also protects me from getting caught doing more stupid shit.

I walk back out onto the dance floor. It's a slow song playing now, very romantic. Dude is singing about following the girl around, watching every move she makes, every breath she takes... Reminds me of me! Hey, are these people sure this is a love song they're dancing to? Kareem and Mo seem to think so.

I spot them first, my new chocolate duo, dancing

together in a tight embrace. They're swaying to the slow song and he's taking every chance to kiss her neck, whisper in her ear, and grab handfuls of that booty. I need to get in closer to hear what they're talking about, so I stroll over and stand right next to them.

"Come on, baby," Kareem says. "You know you want to."

"Nooo," Mo slurs drunkenly. "I'm having fun."

"Babe, it's right down the street. Come on, you really want to stay here and dance to this cracka' music?"

"I don't know..."

"We'd have the whole place to ourselves. My brother won't be back till next week. Come on, baby. Let's go have some fun."

He continues to kiss her and squeeze her, ramping up his efforts to try and get into her pants. I have to admit, homeboy's got game. I can't hear all of what they're saying, as it's loud in here and a lot of their conversation is little romantic whispers, but I get the gist. Kareem's brother has a place nearby. Kareem wants to take Mo there so he can take advantage of her. Got it.

Finally, it looks like Kareem's charms are starting to work. Mo giggles and concedes to his desires, biting her lip in that way that says, *Yeah baby, I'm ready to fuck!* So homeboy leads her across the dance floor to where the others are, and naturally, I follow.

Stephanie is grooving to the music by herself, while nearby, Parker is also dancing by himself. But since they're relatively close, in his mind they're dancing together. Fucking pitiful. Can't wait to slaughter this cheeseball. Richard and Noelle are sitting close to the dance floor, enjoying drinks and talking while watching the others boogie down.

Kareem comes up to Richard and leans down to shout in his ear.

"Yo, we're gonna take off!"

"What?" Richard shouts.

"I said we're gonna take off!" he says even louder.

"Bro, what the hell? We're just getting started here! We're partying all fucking night, dude!"

"We'll be back!" Kareem shouts. "My brother's got a place just a few blocks down. We're gonna go get us some..." he turns to look back at Mo and smiles, "... privacy. Look, we'll just meet you back at your house in a couple hours! Okay?"

Richard shakes his head and laughs, "You dog."

They bump fists. There's an understanding. Guy code.

I watch as they all say their goodbyes, not knowing it will be for the last time. Kareem and Mo head for the door, arm in arm, and of course I follow right behind. All right, big boy, let's see if you can get you some of that chocolate cake before Marvin turns out the lights.

Welp, looks like Mr. Football Star is getting himself some chocolate cake.

I'm looking through a window of a second story apartment, and they are doing the nasty right there on Kareem's brother's bed. He's got her bent over and is giving it to her hard from behind, causing that huge mass of curly fries up front to shake and jiggle. I can't help but laugh.

I'm pretty lucky having access to this window. Yes, it's a second-floor apartment, but there's a little hill on this side of the building, and with that plus my obvious height, I can look right in. I do have to get in there somehow, but I need to wait till they're done. Meantime, I enjoy the show, and my little drone friends are hovering around watching too, so to everyone back home seeing this on TV, you're welcome.

Soul Brotha here is a big mound of lean, sweaty muscles and jheri-curl, while Curly Fries is all jiggles. I certainly don't mind seeing those big, brown sugar titties swishing around. They keep going at it hard and heavy while I plot my next moves. Finally, their moaning and groaning reaches a climax, he dumps his oysters, and they both fall down onto the sheets, panting for breath. Bravo.

A few feet away is the apartment's patio, which I can also reach from the hill I'm standing on. That's my ticket inside. But I have to think of a diversion, something to split them up. Something to... Hey wait, just as I'm thinking it, I see Kareem sit up on the bed and grab the rotary phone beside him.

"Who you calling, baby?" Mo asks.

"My boy, Gary. Score us some chronic!"

"Mmm, I can't... smoke nothin'... Already so... fucked up..."

"Gary? My man! It's Kareem!" His homeboy answers and they begin to chat and laugh. Kareem orders some weed and apparently Gary will be here in less than ten minutes. Good. I hate it when dealers keep you waiting.

Kareem hops up and starts getting dressed while Mo just writhes and groans on the sweat-soaked bedspread. Damn, that black mamba must really run deep. Somehow, I don't think your brother will appreciate coming home to his bedroom being turned into your little love nest, Kareem. Of course, he'll probably be more pissed coming home to find you both murdered, but still.

I walk to the patio a few feet away. The railing comes up to mid-chest on me, so it's pretty easy to just hop, push myself up, then swing my feet over. Boom, now I'm on the patio. I'm able to see in to the kitchen and living room through the sliding glass doors. At first, there's nothing to see. All the lights are off and there's no movement.

But then the bedroom door opens and Kareem comes into the living room, pants and shoes already on, now pulling on his t-shirt. I see Mo in the bed behind him, perfectly content to lay there in post-fuck bliss.

"Yeah, that's cool, baby," Kareem says to her. I can barely hear through the walls, so I press my ear against the window. "I'mma step outside and wait for my boy. If you want, you can take a shower before we go back out."

"Mmm, I don't wanna go back out," Mo slurs, burying her face into the pillows.

"Oh, come on," he laughs, "we partying tonight!"

"Mmm, we can just party here, you and me... Fuck all them honkeys..."

I chuckle to myself. Just the word *honkey*, it always makes me laugh.

Kareem slips his jacket on and leaves through the front door. Perfect. If I time this right, my plan will work brilliantly. I've got the girl by herself and I've got the gun ready to go. I watch for a minute before Mo finally drags her big ass out of bed and stumbles into the bathroom. Good, time to boogie.

I try to open the sliding door, but it's locked. I could break the window, but she might hear it. Then again, she might not. Maybe she's in the shower already. Or maybe it would be quieter to break the door frame rather than breaking a bunch of glass and have it falling all over the floor. Okay, so I slowly apply increasing pressure on the door, pushing against the locking mechanism. Finally, I hear a *pop* and feel a *crunch,* and presto, baby. I'm in.

I duck my head down to step through the sliding door and into the dark living room. Ah yes, I hear the shower running, good. Why not see if Soul Brotha's brotha has anything to drink here? I'm fucking parched. So I find the fridge and look to see what's in stock. Carton of orange juice, oh hell yeah! I pick it up and it feels about three-quarters full. Perfect. I open the spout and just guzzle that whole fucking thing. Ahhh, that hit the spot. Now, where was I?

Oh right, my next victim. I toss the empty juice carton aside and head for the bedroom. The sound of the shower stops and I hear Mo step out, so I pause by the bedroom door. Sitting there on the bed is her wig. Her big, red, ridiculous, curly fries wig. I shake my head.

I hide behind the door and peek in, watching as she walks out of the bathroom, tying a white robe around her waist. Dang girl, now I see why you wear the wig! What the hell is this nappy-looking wasp's nest you got on top of your head? Poor thing.

She goes to her purse and pulls out a small squeeze

bottle of lotion, then starts rubbing it onto her legs. Her back is to me. I duck my head down and creep inside. Closer... closer. Every slow step I take, I cringe, waiting for the floorboards to give me away, but it doesn't happen. I come right up behind her, but she doesn't notice. She reaches for her wig, but it's already in my hand. She feels around the bedspread for it, then finally turns around.

Here I am, baby.

Her eyes open wide and her jaw drops as she looks up at all my sexiness. I hand the wig to her. She finally screams, and I mean at the top of her lungs. Before she can run or try anything, I grab the collar of her robe and hurl her across the room. She crashes into a chest of drawers topped with a mirror, and that thing fucking shatters.

Curly Fries collapses onto the floor, little shards of mirror sticking out of her hands and face. She trembles and gasps, looking up at me as I step closer. I smile, showing her my new pearly whites.

"Hello," I say pleasantly.

I'm about to just grab her and find some clever way to kill her, but I stop myself. No, Marvin. Remember the secondary mission. So I pick up her purse and start rummaging through it. I find her driver's license and pull it out. I look at her, then at the photo on the license. Yeah, it does look like her.

"Tell me your name," I say.

"W-w-what...?"

"What's your name!"

"M-M-Missouri!" she squeals, terrified.

"What's your last name, Missouri?"

"W-Watson!"

"What's your address?"

"F-f-fifty three Walnut Street!"

Okay, she's got the basics right. Let's see how she reacts to some more questions. I toss her ID and pull out my little notepad, quickly turning to the page where I transcribed her bio from the dossier.

"Where do you go to school?" I ask.

She answers correctly.

"Where were you born?"

She answers correctly.

"What are your hobbies?"

Once again, she answers correctly. Hmm. I stop and think to myself as she remains on the floor, trembling in fear and looking up at me, confused. What exactly am I getting at? Why wouldn't she know the basic facts about herself? Do I suspect she's some kind of actress playing a part? No, come on. Nobody signs on to play a character and actually get murdered for real. Still, I feel the need to keep testing her, find out just how deep she goes.

"What kind of person are you?" I ask. Now she looks completely stumped.

"W-what? I don't u-underst—"

"What kind of person are you? Are you honest an' loyal? Are you a bitch? What do you think about? What are you into?"

"I-I don't know..." I know, that's a lot to unpack, quite a few questions there. A little difficult to answer when you're drunk and bleeding on the floor and a giant psychopath is towering over you. "I-I guess I'm a nice person...?"

"More," I say, "give me more. What makes you unique? Tell me somethin' interestin' about yourself."

"W-what? I-I don't..."

Okay, I've had enough of this shit. I don't know where I'm going with this and she don't have a clue anyway. Hell, even if she was stone-cold sober and not terrified, she still probably couldn't think of anything interesting about herself. She's just a shallow bubble-head of a person. She lives to party, get fucked, and get fucked up. All right then, little missy, time to get fucked up.

I pocket my notepad and grab Mo by the back of the neck, lifting her up off the floor. She screams and flails. I grab her wig off the bed. Gotta think of some cool way to kill her with the wig. Hmm. I imagine making her choke on it, but how can a person choke on a wi... Aha, I've got it!

I march into the bathroom, Mo in one hand, the monstrosity of a wig in the other. She's kicking and howling and scratching real hard. See, what did I say? Black people *really* seem to not like being horribly murdered. Well, sorry honey, but it's time for a little poetic injustice. So I drop her to the floor and snatch up the toilet plunger.

"You crazy cracka' motherfucker! My boyfriend will be back and he's gonna kick yo' ass! Kareem! Kareeeeeem, heeeeelp!"

I take the wig and place it on the end of the plunger handle.

I yank Mo off her feet again, kicking and screaming of course.

I stuff the enormous, curly wig into her open mouth. Her eyes bug out.

Then it's just the simple process of using the plunger to jam the wig deeper and deeper down her mouth hole. She hits me, scratches, kicks, but it's no use. I'm using a wooden rod to force a giant, red, curly-fry wig to asphyxiate as well as destroy the bones and tissues in her skull and throat.

First, her lower jaw snaps off its hinges as it's forced to open way wider than it's designed to. The pink flesh of her tongue and larynx rips away as I feed her those curly fries. Her eyes bug out beet-red. Bloody foam and spittle. Her throat stretches to three times its normal size as I finally mash the entire thing in there, nothing but the filthy, rubber sucker left sticking out of her mouth.

She spasms and collapses, nice and dead.

Oh yeah, I can dig it, baby.

But now it's time for the really fun part of the plan.

I take out the gun that's been in my pocket this whole time, carefully placing it on the floor next to Mo's hand, so it looks like she tried to use it. I open the drawer in the bedside stand so it looks like she found the gun in there. Perfect. Now there's just one thing left to do.

I sit down on the bed and pick up the phone. I dial 911.

The dispatcher answers and I do my best to sound upset.

"Yes, hello! Police?" I gasp. "A woman's been murdered in here! And there's a Black man outside with a gun! Send the police *now!*"

CHAPTER 12

NOW I JUST WAIT FOR Soul Brotha to come back in and take the bait. I go into the bedroom closet where I have a clear view of the front door, and hide. I kneel down and slide a few jackets on hangers in front of me. Any minute now, Kareem will come back in, find Mo a little worse for wear, and... well, fingers crossed.

Come on... come on... Oop! Here we go!

Kareem struts through the front door, happily whistling a tune.

"I'm back, babe!" he says, tossing his jacket onto a chair.

Sexual Chocolate makes sure to check himself in the mirror, primps his hair, checks his teeth. I watch as he plops down onto the couch, pulling out a plastic baggie full of some primo smoke. Mmm, nice, it's been a while. Might just have to get me some of that. He goes about rolling a joint, oblivious to what's transpired in the other room over the last five minutes. He must think she's still in bed asleep. Oh boy, this is gonna be good. Soul Brotha lights the doobie and stands back up.

"Babe?" he says, coming towards the bedroom. "C'mon, wake up."

Kareem comes to the bedroom and I huddle as far back into the closet as I can, staying in the shadows. He puts his hand on the door and slowly pushes it open.

"Babe? You wanna hit this?"

He comes into the room. Turns the light on. Doesn't see it yet.

Come a little closer, bud. You'll see her feet on the other side of the bed.

"Babe?"

Come on... Come on...

He finally starts walking towards the bathroom, and boom, he sees her. Kareem stops dead in his tracks and his eyes pop right out of his head. He drops the joint to the floor and his hands start shaking. It takes him a second to process what he's seeing — his girlfriend sprawling across the floor, dead, her head and throat ripped apart, and a toilet plunger sticking out of her mouth — then finally screams.

"MO!! MOOOOO!!!"

He runs to her, scooping her up and holding her in his arms. The expression on his face is priceless as he blubbers and whines, I love it. Come on, buddy, notice the gun. Come on... Hm, I might have to give him a little encouragement. Now comes the fun part.

I stand up and thrust the jackets and hangers that were shielding me out of the way, sending them flying into the room. I duck my head down and step through the door, doing my best to be scary and imposing and terrify-ing. I puff up my chest and shoulders, give him my best mad-dog eyes, and stomp forward.

Kareem falls back onto his ass, yelping like a little bitch and dropping his girlfriend's corpse back to the floor. His eyes are full of dread as he sees me, recognizes me, and understands what's about to happen to him. Or at least he thinks he does... Come on, notice the gun!

I continue to stalk forward menacingly and he scoots back.

Finally, he sees the gun and reflexively grabs it.

I step towards him, throwing the bed aside, smashing the dresser and bedside table for added dramatic effect. And it works. Kareem scurries to his feet and runs for the door. But not before popping off a couple shots at me.

Blam! Blam!

Now, how could he have known that I'd loaded that gun with blanks? Sure, I can get killed and come back three times per clash, but still. It's never fun to get shot in the chest, so I'd rather play it safe and not even give him a chance. Kareem just assumes his shots missed me and bolts out of the bedroom, then finally out the front door.

Yes! Okay, here we go!

I rush out of the bedroom and go to the kitchen window, where I can see the front entrance and the street outside. I hear police sirens growing louder as they approach. I wait... I wait... Finally, I see Kareem stumble from the front door of the complex, a gun in his hand, his girlfriend's blood streaked on his clothes.

I see the red and blue lights. They're here!

A half-dozen police cruisers screech to a halt, forming a semi-circle around the raving, wild-eyed Black man. The doors fly open and an arsenal of guns is trained on him in a second.

"Drop the weapon!"

"Drop it now!"

The cops are all shouting and poor Kareem is just in a daze. He's trembling, blood on his face, gun in his hand... Oh yeah, he's in shock. Here we go... Come on...

After repeatedly commanding Kareem to drop the gun, they open fire.

Blam! Blam! Boom! Chk-Koom! Kapow!

A combination of 9mm, .357 magnum and 12-gauge buckshot peppers Kareem up real good. He does that retarded dumb-fuck dance that people do when they're getting shredded by gunfire. Finally, with his blood and guts and brains splattered across the front entrance of the apartment complex, Soul Brotha drops his gun.

YESSSS!!!!

That couldn't have possibly gone any better! I fucking nailed that one, baby! *Woooo!!!* Take that, Larry! I set that shit up and paid it right the fuck off! He took that bait just like I knew he would, and then the police took the bait, and oh! it just worked out so fucking perfect! *Woo!!*

Happy Marvin dance!

I do a little jig, spin around, shake my booty. I jump up in the air and click my heels together. I hold my arms open and take my bows as the hummingbird-fucker drones broadcast the feed back to the ravenous sickos watching back home. That's right, everyone, *I'm* the fucking champion! Greatest of all time, bitches.

Alrighty. Time to ramp things up.

I need to get back to the club, follow the rest of our lucky contestants home, and finish up my little performance. But first... that joint is still smoldering on the bedroom floor. So I grab that fucker and take a nice, big drag. Hold that shit in. Let it out nice and slow... Oh, yeah...

Gonna finish smoking this little baby as I walk back to the club. Fuck it. I'm gonna get fucking *loaded*. After all, it is party time!

CHAPTER 13

BY THE TIME I make it back to the club, it looks like my little secret is out. Somebody found my date, the poor boy I left in the bathroom with his head lodged in the toilet. Or maybe they found the headless clown I left outside in the phone booth. Either way, the whole place is surrounded by police and fire department personnel, and the party-goers are all filing out through the doors. Party's over, folks. Oh, well.

I lift the joint to my mouth for another hit and there's nothing left but a little roach. Maybe if I had full lips that actually fit together and fingers smaller than bratwursts, I might be able to hold this little fucker and hit it. But it's just too much work at this point, so I flick it away. I'm feeling good already, warm and fuzzy. Had me some liquor, now some smoky-smoke, oh yeah, baby. Feeling goooood.

But what's happened to our lucky contestants?

I remember them saying their plan was to meet back at Richard's house anyway, so I can only assume that they're walking in that direction. As the crowd of costumed twerps disperses, I go back to the coastline, walking along that stretch that will lead to Richard's house. There's still a few other people here and there, some walking to their cars and starting them up, others splitting off onto side streets. Pretty soon they're all gone, and I find myself alone on this walkway. Or is this a bike path? Oh, whatever.

Up ahead, I finally see them—Richard, Noelle, Stephanie and Parker. Yup, all heading back to the house just like I thought. Richard has his arm around Noelle, while the other two trail behind, Stephanie making sure to keep her distance from Chunky Pirate. They look out at the ocean, admiring the lights of San Fran Bay, passing all the docks in the harbor. All the boats are tied up for the night and only a couple old fishermen are still around, finishing up their chores before going home.

Mmm, maybe I'll just steal a boat and go do some fishing...

Richard and Noelle whisper to each other, cuddling, flirting.

"Hey, guys," Richard says to the two behind them, "you in the mood for some ice cream?"

Parker perks up. "Yeah, sure!" he says.

"Okay," Stephanie shrugs. She's just over this whole night.

"Cool," Richard stops, turning to face the others, his arm still around Noelle's shoulders. "You don't mind if me and *Alice* head on ahead and meet you later at the house, do you? I have an anniversary gift for my special lady."

"Wait, you mean... oh, no. Please..." Stephanie realizes what's happening.

"Here," Richard says, pulling out his wallet and dispensing some cash into Parker's hand, "there's twenty bucks. You two guys go get some ice cream, huh?"

"Sure!" Parker gleefully shouts.

"Noelle," Stephanie begs, grabbing her friend's arm and giving her a hard look. "Please don't leave me. Please..."

"Come on, Steph. You two can get to know each other a bit."

Stephanie just glares at her.

"Yeah, Steph," Parker says, "Baskin Robbins is just three blocks up that way. I'll protect you!" Fat Boy pulls out his plastic pirate sword and puffs his chest out.

Stephanie sighs and smiles, but I can tell... she's screaming inside.

Richard begins pulling Noelle away back toward his house, leaving Parker and Stephanie behind as they say their goodbyes. They stand there in silence. Alrighty... this is awkward.

"Well then, m'lady," Parker says, sticking out his elbow like he expects her to walk arm-in-arm with him. "May I escort you to the ice cream parlor?"

"Mmm, look, that's okay. I'm trying to watch my figure."

"Oh come on, your figure looks great! You're beautiful..."

Parker steps closer and tries to put his hands on her shoulders, but she pulls away. She's not into you, dude. Come on.

"Look, Parker. You're a nice guy, okay? I just don't... I just..."

Parker deflates like a balloon. "You hate me."

"I didn't say that."

"You don't have to say it. I know," he says, storming off into the darkness.

"Parker, where are you going?"

"I'm going to get some ice cream! By myself! Have a nice night!"

Awww, poor baby. Rejection don't feel good, does it? Maybe don't go after girls who are way out of your league? I don't know, just a thought. In any case, Stephanie sighs and shakes her head, watching as Parker fades into the distance. She turns and looks out at the ocean sparkling in the moonlight. Ahhh, so pretty, better take a closer look.

I watch from the shadows as Barbie strolls over to the docks, finding a railing to lean on and look out at the ocean. Here we go: pretty girl, nobody else around. This is it. I tip-toe from one tree to another, hiding in the darkness as I draw in closer. Carefully, I step around leaves and twigs, not wanting to make a single sound. I finally get within a few feet of her when she suddenly decides to keep moving.

From the railing on the coastline, Stephanie walks further out onto the docks. She strolls past fishing boats and house boats, across the creaky, wooden boards, and towards the end of the pier. She sits down on the edge, letting her feet dangle, looking out at the stars and the waves and the glittery lights of San Francisco.

I move in closer, feeling the cool ocean breeze on my skin, breathing in the smell of sea water and feeling... not so good. Shit. I probably should've stopped with the whiskey. Adding pot to the mix may have been a mistake, because now that warm and fuzzy feeling is starting to turn hot and sweaty. Feels like I'm floating, like I'm spinning. Shit! Come on, Marvin! Hold it together! I move in closer... closer.

Just a few feet from my target and the dock betrays me. The old, water-logged boards creak under my weight and Stephanie instantly jerks around. She sees me and her jaw drops. As a reflex, she jumps to her feet and spins around to face me, but she's right on the edge of the pier and suddenly finds herself desperately teetering to regain balance. Her arms flail and spin but it's obvious she's about to fall into the water.

I shoot out a hand and grab her glitzy jacket by the lapels, pulling her back in towards me. She swats at me and gasps in horror as she takes a good look at my pretty face.

"No, please! No!!" she begs and pleads.

I lift her off her feet, pulling her face right up to mine.

Now would be the perfect time for a catchy one-liner. So I open my mouth and try to think of something clever. But the world is spinning and my mouth is now watering, and what comes out is most definitely not a clever one-liner.

Nope, instead I blow chunks all over her fucking face. It's a good one too. I mean, it's full-blown projectile vomit, a proprietary blend of cheap whiskey, expensive indica, the double-bacon burger and fries I ate earlier in the day and a few gallons of bile and stomach acid. It keeps going. And going.

Stephanie screams and spits as it splashes all over her fucking face, feebly swatting at my chest as I hang on to her collar. The flow of puke stops. I gasp for breath a few seconds, hanging on, pukey spittle dripping from my lips.

Just seeing it and smelling it grosses me out, and I feel my stomach rumbling again.

Annnnnd round two! *Fwoooooossshhhhh!!*

"Ahhhhh!!! Ptah! Pffffff!! S-stop! Please!! Ahhhhhh!!!"

I have to say, I love the way she screams and tries to spit it away as a steady stream of slimy funk sprays into her mouth, up her nose, into her eyes, hair, fucking everywhere. Finally, I let her go and she drops to the dock, a big, slimy pile of barf, gasping for air.

I put my hands on my hips and catch my breath, pacing around. Ahhhh, what a relief. I smile and look down at her.

"Hoo! That's better," I say. "Ughhh, sorry about that."

She just sits there, all pukey, quivering, in shock.

I remember my second objective and snatch up her purse, pulling out the wallet. I find her driver's license and pull it out, tossing the purse aside.

"Okay," I say, beginning my quiz, "what's your name?"

Stephanie just sits there, shaking.

"Come on, come on. What's your name?"

She just sits there, shaking.

"What's your address?"

Same shit. Hm, I don't think I'm gonna get much out of this one. She's drunk and terrified and drenched in psycho-vomit, and I think the shock has taken her. She's checked out, no one behind the wheel. She won't be answering questions any time soon. Okay, well so much for my test. I'll just finish up with Barbie Doll and move on.

My first instinct is to grab her and do a head squeeze, rip her head off, or something like that, but honestly, I don't even want to touch her. She's fucking soaked in barf stew. Ew, that's gross. So instead, I look around for a tool. One of the docked fishing boats has a bunch of tools still sitting out on the deck: fishing poles, lures, nets, poles, and a collection of small knives.

One blade, however, catches my eye. It brings me back to the days of fishing with my dad. It's a Galivan Cane machete, basically just a regular machete except there's a mean-looking hook on one side of the blade. I remember my daddy using one edge to cut the fish's heads off, then flipping it over and using the hook to drag the carcasses, or to hook nets, lines and so on.

So I step on board, scoop up the old chopper, and hop back up onto the dock. Stephanie is still there crumpled on the dock, a big puddle of quivering, trembling vomit. Time to just get rid of her good and quick, using this new tool to keep my distance. She's so deep in shock, she doesn't even look up as I approach.

I flip the machete in my hand, angling the hook just where I want it. With one good, chopping motion, I whip that hook right into Barbie's eye socket, popping that juicy ball of goo and penetrating into her brain. Her body tenses and spasms, and she starts making these cute little guttural-grunting noises like she's taking a shit.

Using the machete to keep a good distance from her, I angle the hook to drag her to the very edge of the pier. With a good flick of the handle, I shrug the hook out of her bleeding eye socket and let her tumble into the ocean. Buh-bye. If you're not dead yet, the combination of massive brain trauma and being submerged in the ocean while in shock should do the trick.

I probably should've said something clever right there. Something like, "How about a nice dip?" or "Gotta keep your eye on the prize." Larry would've said something cool like that. Hm. In any case, my work here is done. Now I have to catch up with that fat fuck Parker, and I'm taking my new toy with me.

Walking back down the pier, one boat suddenly catches my eye. It's bigger than the others, and there's more gear on board too. There's lobster baskets, big nets, coolers, rigging gear, you name it. There's a grill on board along with a table and chairs, a little boom box, and plenty of other personal items. This isn't just a fishing boat, this is someone's house boat. Some clothes have been left on a line to dry. Big clothes. Man, those look like they might just fit even me!

I step onto the deck, careful not to make a sound. Looks like the owner is probably asleep inside or away somewhere. Either way, I tip-toe across the deck, looking to see if I can find anything cool. And then I see something. I stop. Stop dead in my tracks. Everything goes quiet and still.

The clouds part and the moonlight shines down on the deck. A choir of angels begins to sing. My heart swells up with an unfamiliar feeling, and I almost start to cry. I step in closer, doubting my own eyes. But no, what I'm seeing is really real, really there.

It's a pair of fishing boots. A very *big* pair of fishing boots.

They're green and yellow, heavy-duty rubber, old

and scuffed, made for a working man. I pick one up and study it. Could it be the right size? Is it actually possible? Convinced I must be dreaming, I sit down, put the machete aside, and slip my foot into the boot.

Perfect. Fucking. Fit.

No way. This is too good to be true. I have to try the other one on too. There's got to be something wrong, some catch. I grab the second boot, take a deep breath, and slip my other foot into it... Perfect. Fucking. Fit. I stand up, absolutely flabbergasted. I walk around, testing them out. They're ever-so-slightly tight, but not uncomfortable, and they give off a slight squeak when I walk, but so what?

I've found a pair of shoes that fits me!!!

Now I really am crying. For the first time in a long time, I feel complete. My toes are snug and warm. I have a cool machete. I'm happy... I'm actually happy! I'd better get out of here before the owner of this boat wakes up. Sure, I could just go kill him first, but no. Not you, brother. Not you, fellow big boy. You did me a solid.

No, the person I really need to kill right now is on his way to stuff ice cream into his fat mouth, so I hop out of the boat and land on the dock, ready to go after him. Ahhh, these shoes feel good to walk in, gives me an extra spring in my step! Oh yeah, baby, I'm ready to turn up the heat!

CHAPTER 14

OH, Parker! P-P-P-Parkerrr! Yoo hoo!

I hit the gas a little, stalking in the direction I saw Fat Pirate Boy go. These new boots feel good and it sure is nice to not feel rough concrete on my feet, but they don't help the fact that my cardio is shit. Boots or no boots, I'm starting to feel out of breath, so I pace myself. I see people pass me on the sidewalk, some wearing costumes, and I wave and snarl at them, playing the part. They eat it up.

A couple blocks ahead, I think I see him. Yup, Porky Pirate, that's you, cutting through the park to get to the ice cream shop. I follow him quietly, stepping out of the streetlights and into the shadows of the park. Ahhh, this is where I'm at home. Nice and dark and barely anyone around. I see Parker up ahead, kicking the ground as he walks and grumbling to himself.

"Bitch," grumble grumble, "fuck you," grumble grumble.

Then I hear him start to cry. Ugh, come on. I don't know what I want to do more, horribly murder this kid or sit down and counsel him, help him achieve and actualize his goals and drea... what the hell am I thinking? Still so drunk and stoned, head thick in a fog. Shake it off, Marvin! You're murdering the little shit stain.

Parker The Pirate continues along the dark pathway, through some trees, winding up and down little hills. It's really pretty here. Another person walks past, but there are so few, I can easily find a window to strike. I watch as my target reaches the top of a hill, then suddenly stops, gazing off towards the sound of distant music.

"Oh, man..." he says, melting down into tears. "I wanted to see them so ba-ha-ha-haaaaad!"

I look in that direction and yup, way across town there's the amphitheater where his favorite band, The Grateful Dead, is playing. Parker sees a park bench and plops down on it, crying like a little pussy. I know, buddy, it's too late to see your show. But think of it this way, things are about to get a whole lot worse for you, and the concert will be the least of your concerns.

Without further ado, I walk up to the bench and sit down right next to Parker. He flinches, making a cute little squeal as he sees me.

"Hello, Parker," I say with a smile, sticking the machete into the dirt.

He starts to scream and bolt, but my hand slaps down on the back of his neck, holding his chunky ass down. Every time he tries to scream I just apply a little pressure to the delicate bones in his neck, and he quiets right the fuck down.

"Oh, God! P-please..."

I pull out my little notepad, find the notes I wrote down about him.

"What's your full name?" I ask.

"W-what?!"

I squeeze harder. He hisses in agony.

"Ahhh! Parker! P-Parker Andrews!"

"What's your address?"

"Nnng! Fifteen Winterlane Drive! S-San Francisco! Ahh!"

I need to take a different tact here. I don't know what I'm doing or what I'm looking for. I guess, some hint that these people aren't who they say they are. Like, has David Black put a spell on me and this is all in my mind? Or am I in some sort of computer stimulation? There's no way this is real. It's all just too crazy, too convenient. Right. I need to ask some questions that aren't obvious.

"Peanut butter. Creamy or chunky?" I ask.

Parker looks at me, utterly baffled. I squeeze a little.

"Chunky!" he says.

"Favorite flavor of ice cream?"

"Oh, chocolate-chip mint, dude!"

"Mm. That is a good one, yeah." I think for a minute. "What kind of a *person* are you, Parker?" I give him a long look.

He contemplates, then gets all teary-eyed and says, "I'm a piece of shit. I'm fat. I'm ugly. I'm not even talented or anything. I'm not rich, I got a little dick... I'm a loser! Okay? I'm lonely and pissed off and jealous! I'm never gonna have a hot girlfriend, nobody's ever gonna love me..." now he's flat-out sobbing again. "Okay? Is that what you want to hear, you fucking bastard?"

"Tell me your name again."

"Dude, I already told you! Ronnie Br—" and then he stops, a baffled look coming over his face. He blinks, and it's gone. "Parker. I'm Parker Andrews."

I squeeze harder, pulling him right up to my face.

"Aha! What was that? What was that other name?"

"W-what name?"

"That name you started to say! Ronnie! Is that your name?"

"No! I'm Parker! I swear!"

"Then why did you start to say Ronnie?"

"I don't know! Please, I'm sorry!! I don't wanna die!!!"

Yes you do, buddy. Everything you're telling me, whatever your name is, tells me you'd rather be dead. Well, turns out I can help with that.

I relax my grip a little. Smile.

"So, you like the Grateful Dead, huh?"

Parker chuckles a little. "Y-yeah. I do."

"That's them playin' across town, right? I can hear it, see the lights. That's it over there, right?" I point a finger across the city, where the spotlights at the Marin County Amphitheater are spinning and the shitty music can be heard from here.

"Yeah, that's it," he whimpers. "My friends didn't want to go, and besides, I don't have money for a ticket anyway."

"Hm," I say, contemplating the physics of what I have in mind, "maybe there's a way you can still see them tonight."

"Huh? How?" He perks up, looking at me with hope in his eyes.

"Well, did you know that a human head remains conscious for up to thirty seconds after decapitation?"

I wait for that look of recognition in his eyes.

It takes a second, then there it is. He knows.

"Oh, no!" he begs, "No no! Please!"

I stand up, carrying Parker with me. I pick up my machete. He continues to scream and cry, punching and kicking. Actually, his boots are hurting my knees a little bit. Fucker. I change my grip, moving from the back of his neck to grabbing a fistful of hair right on top.

"No, please! *Noooooo!!*"

"Enjoy the show!" I say and lash out with the blade.

One hard chop and Fat Fuck's head pops right off and is now dangling in my grip. His pathetic, flabby body collapses to the ground, spewing and spraying hot blood out of his bitch hole. The blood splashes against my boots, and I feel a sense of peace and calm, a satisfaction in not having to feel this dumb fuck's blood drying between my toes.

I look at his face immediately after and sure enough, his eyes are still looking around. Good, he's still conscious! I have only a few seconds, so I have to act fast.

I size up the distance. Ready my throwing arm.

I take a step back, do an underhand swing, and launch that fucker up into the sky. It takes only a few seconds, but I watch at Pirate Boy's head sails through the air, going, going... bam! I see it disappear as it falls inside the open-air arena. I throw up my arms and celebrate like I just hit a touchdown in the Superbowl.

Now, there's no way to be certain, but I like to imagine that as young Parker's head flew through the sky, rapidly losing blood and on the verge of unconsciousness and brain death, that somehow, he still caught just a little of the show. Like, as his head started to plummet inside, just before it collided into the ground, or maybe cracked right into someone else's head, he did see just a little bit.

I wonder if anyone in there even notices. Like, maybe it lands on top of a speaker and nobody sees it until tomorrow when the roadies are breaking down their gear. Or maybe it hits the floor right where people are, but they're all so stoned and it's so loud that nobody notices. They just keep dancing, kicking Parker's head around, it ends up in a puddle of beer and cigarette butts and Fernando the cleaning man finds it tomorrow afternoon. Or even better, if it hit Stoner Claus in the face right there on stage!

Hey, that's what you get having an open-air theater! Might want to put a dome on that sucker soon. Just saying. In any case, that was weird with the other name thing. Ronnie? What could it mean? Whatever it is, I'm paying attention and I'm not letting it slide. If The BMC is fucking me somehow, I'm gonna burn the whole damn thing down.

CHAPTER 15

BACK AT RICHARD'S house on Seaview Avenue.

I'm crouched in the bushes outside, peeping through the window of the master bedroom as Alice appears to be tumbling deep into the rabbit hole with the Cheshire Cat. Or is he the Mad Hatter? Whoever Richard is in this scenario, Noelle is Alice, and Alice is getting fucked. Well, they're groovin' slowly to some easy-listening shit, so I'm sure they'd call it making love. Gag me. In any case, little Noelle does have some nice perkies on her and I don't mind that one little bit.

Since they're occupado and nobody else is around, there's no better time than now to sneak in there. Hopefully I can find an unlocked door, otherwise I don't mind a little breaking and entering. So, I begin slinking—well, the closest a seven-foot, four hundred-pound man can get to slinking—around the perimeter of the home. Mmmm, that jacuzzi is calling my name... no, Marvin. Focus.

I start checking doors when suddenly, a familiar feeling comes over me, a tingling and a pulling. Oh, shit! I take out my stopwatch and check the time. The digital clock counts down 3...2...1... No! Second period is over! I lost track of time!

In an instant, those fuckers yank me back through.

. . .

I plop down into Hell again, back at the Grand Malavista Arena. Fuck. The crowd roars and lights flash and spin. I hold my hands up high and pump my fists, playing to my legions of fans. I see Larry sitting there, talking some shit. Don't worry, I'll hear all your little commentary when I rewatch this later at home. Cunt.

Jim and the boys rush up to greet me.

"Looking good, man! Looking good!" Jim says, giving me some water.

"Hey!" calls out a voice I recognize from behind me.

It's El Presidente David Black, and he's coming this way. He does not look happy. The bald man in the black suit pushes past Jim and gets right in my face.

"What are you doing in there, Marvin?" he says.

"Just doin' my job."

"Oh yeah? What's this checking ID's shit? What's with the twenty questions?"

"I just wanna get to know them better, that's all."

"Why? Marvin, the fans are here to see you *kill* these assholes, not to listen to them talk about their feelings! That shit isn't good for business! Now, you already got one penalty; want to go for two?"

"Penalty?" I perk up, getting mad. "What penalty?"

"Just get back in there and do your job, Brumlow! Got it?"

He gives me a hard look. Watch it, buddy. I don't care who you are, but I nod and play along. Mr. Black huffs and turns away, returning to his box seats. I look back at Jim, who's busying himself by toweling me off.

"You look good to *me* out there, man," Jim says, smacking his gum. "Great kills. Love the boots, too!"

I smile. "Thanks, Jim."

"Two more to go," he says, slapping my shoulder. "You know what to do!"

Indeed, I do. Let me at 'em.

THE BREAK IS OVER AND I STEP BACK THROUGH THE veil. Hello, Earth. Again.

Okay, this is it, time to finish these last two off and go home. First thing I have to do is ensure that they ain't going nowhere or calling no one. I start by going back to the front and slashing the tires of both the Bug and the van. Then it's around to the side to cut the phone lines. *Snip.* All done. I try the front door just in case. Locked, of course.

I go around back again and trot up onto the deck. I try the slider. Locked. Hm, I could continue checking around the house, but let's face it, all the doors are going to be locked. And besides, I have a better idea anyway. Time to do a little fishing.

The first thing you need to do if you want to catch a fish is have a good lure. I have to get Richie Rich to come to me. So instead of trying to break in nice and quiet, I take the opposite approach. I punch right through the fucking window. *Skeeesshh!* It's nice and loud. I reach through the hole, unlock the door latch, and slide my way inside. Closing the door behind me, I tip-toe off into the shadows and wait.

A few seconds goes by, then I hear the bedroom door open upstairs.

"What was that?" I hear Noelle ask.

"I don't know..." Richard says. "Hello? Anyone there?"

"Sounds like something broke."

"Stay here. I'll go check it out."

Yes, come to me, little fishy. I peek around a corner, hidden in the shadows, gripping the handle of my new favorite hooked machete. I hear Richard's footsteps as he trots down the stairs. From where he is, I don't think he can see the broken sliding door. Come all the way down, buddy. That's it... that's it...

"Hello?" Richard calls out and comes into view. He's in a pair of boxers and a white t-shirt, obviously thrown on in haste. He clicks on the light as he walks into the living room. He looks around, nervous. Closer, buddy, closer... "Oh, shit."

He finally sees the broken glass, the hole in the door.

I'm ready. The hummingbird fuckers are ready.

Richard runs to the phone and picks it up. Dead. Sorry, dude.

His lips begin to tremble and his face goes white as a sheet. I believe this is where I make my entrance. Puffing my chest out and making my meanest face, I come into the light. The floorboards groan under my boots. Richie Rich turns and finally sees me. He makes this cute little whooping sound and his knees turn to jelly as I stalk right up to him. Ooh, I think I have a good line to say!

"How's it hangin', Dick?" Haha, take that, Larry.

Richard finally screams like a little bitch, paralyzed and unable to run or fight or do anything to preserve his life. I grab him by the throat and lift him off the ground, and his little feet are kicking at me. Adorable.

I hear from upstairs, "Richard? What's wrong?"

It's little miss Alice in Wonderland, running to the top of the stairs and screaming when she finally sees what her boyfriend looks like held up next to a *real man*. Check this out, baby, look what I'm doing to your loverboy now.

I jab the hook of my machete into the right side of his belly, then drag it all the way across to the left. *Slatchtsz-zkkrsshhh!* Very nice, his intestines spill out just as I'd hoped. Richard howls in shock and pain, watching as his hot guts just fucking splash all over his feet. Noelle screams. Fuck it, I'll scream too.

"Yaaaaaaah!!" I scream right in Richard's face and drop him to the floor. He collapses into a pile, desperately stuffing his gizzards back into that big 'ol hole. Meanwhile, I turn to face Noelle with a dripping-red machete and a big, shit-eating grin on my face. She screams and runs back into the bedroom, locking the door. I consider going after her, but I think I'll finish up with Romeo first.

Looks like he's gathered up his guts and is staggering away, going for the back door. Trying to escape. Nnnnnope. I stalk after him. The girl can wait. She can't call out and she'll be too terrified to try and run. Richie Rich sees me coming after him and picks up the pace, causing him to stumble and fall. He smashes face-first into the glass door I already broke, shattering it into a million fucking pieces, and falls onto the back deck, screaming and whining.

I go after him, of course. He's got hundreds of shards of glass embedded in his face, hands, body, fucking everywhere, and I hope each one hurts. He's desperately running into the backyard, both hands holding his guts in. Gotta hand it to him, he's really showing some will. That's it, little buddy, resist. Run. Fight. All makes for a good show.

And now it looks like at the end of the property, it turns into a hill which Richard is able to start scaling down. Shit. Okay, showing a bit *too* much will there, my man. Stop trying so hard. Great, now I have to start walking down a steep slope with trees and rocks and shit. But Richard does me a favor and trips, rolling downhill into the darkness between properties.

He yelps like a little dog as he hits the next level down, his large intestine and stomach and everything just spilled right the fuck out. Looks like he's found the platform with the electric transformer that powers this grid of houses. I jump down and begin to advance, nice and slow, menacing, putting on a show.

The flying cameras close in.

Richard continues to grunt and cry as he drags himself forward. He scoops up his spilled beans and staggers on, all bloody and disgusting and in agony. Where exactly do you think you're gonna go, dude? Around the transformer and all these high-voltage cables? You really think you're gonna get away? You know what, I think I'll just help you along.

I give Richie Rich a good shove in the center of his back.

He flies toward the electric cables. His hands shoot out as a reflex, I guess, and he grabs the cable to stop himself from falling.

FRRRZZZZTTTZTTTKKKXXZZZZZ!!!

Woo! I see sparks flying and smoke fizzling as a ka-jillion fucking volts of electricity shoots through poor Richard's hands, up his arms and into his body, absolutely frying him from the inside out. His eyes have rolled back in his head, mouth gaping open. His arms are turned all charred and black as he continues to convulse and spasm. Yes! Suffer, you prick!

His spilled intestines quiver and cook and fucking rupture and in all my years of dishing out excruciating deaths, I've never seen anything like it. When Richie Rich finally lets go and drops on his ass, his arms look like two burnt matchsticks and his guts look like a platter of charred bar-be-cue. Blood drips from his nose, mouth and ears, oh yeah, and from his eyes, too! This is so cool!

And yet, somehow he's still alive. There's this feeble wheezing coming from his throat, and his chest is still rising and falling. Time to put the final exclamation point on this one. Head squash? Head squash.

I wrap my big hand around Richard's head, my fingers reaching all the way down to his mouth. He begins to scream. I apply force. His skull makes a loud *pop* as I squeeze it good and hard, forcing his skull and brains and eyeballs and nose and teeth and tongue and hair right the fuck out between my fingers. Big, juicy splatter.

The remains of Richard's body falls to the ground, convulsing and steaming. Stinking too! Man, it may look like bar-be-cue, but it smells like ass! However, it looked good and painful and I'm sure the fans back at the arena and those watching at home are all cheering my name right now. That's right, Larry. Suck it.

One more to go, and she'd better not give me any trouble.

CHAPTER 16

THAT LAST ONE took me too long. I've been gone nearly five minutes roasting that poo-poo platter with the douche sauce, and as I march back up to the backyard, around the pool and to the back porch, I worry that Alice in Wonderland has already split. I cut the phone, so I know know she can't call out, which leaves her two options: hide and barricade herself in, or run. But if I've been gone too long, eventually she'd take a chance and make a run for it.

Fingers crossed. I slip back through the broken sliding door and into the dark living room. Everything is quiet. Three of the little cameras follow me, two of them sliding straight through the walls like ghosts. Love when they do that. Actually, it gives me an idea. I wave at the hummingbird fucker closest to me.

"Psst. Hey!" I say, keeping my voice down.

I gesture for it to come closer, and the little dude hums on over. Maybe I can get him to do some of my work for me!

"Listen," I say, whispering to the weird little camera-helicopter thingie, "can you take a quick look around upstairs, then come back and let me know if the girl's still here?" The thing just hovers there, looking at me like a dumb fuck. I'm sure the fans right now are questioning what I'm doing too. Finally, after processing the request, my little hummingbird buddy buzzes up the stairs to search.

Nice. I'm not exactly stealthy, and if she's still here hiding, I want to know where she is before she knows where I am. So let's see if this works. I wonder if this is against the BMC rules, actually. Guess I'll find out.

While I wait, I look around the home, vacantly checking out their family photos and decorations, movies and music and whatnot. And something catches my eye. There's a book on the coffee table, and the picture of the guy on the cover draws me in. He looks like some chipmunk-cheek douchebag with a bowl cut, wearing a pompous suit. Wait, I recognize this guy. The name on the cover, Thompson Wells, PhD. The title, *Into the Depths of Psychosis*.

It's that guy! I keep seeing him talking about me! Every time I do a clash, he's on the TV, or he's being quoted somewhere else... He's part of this, whatever this is, this... weirdness! It's like this book was left out here *for me*. Who is this guy? How is he involved? Fuck, this is weird. Okay, I'm taking this book. I stuff it into the big front pocket in my overalls where it fits good. I'll deal with you later, Doctor Wells.

The hummingbird I sent off is coming back downstairs, so I go to the foot of the steps to meet him. It. Little dude buzzes down til he's eye level with me.

"Well? Is she here?" I ask.

Little dude nods. I mean, it moves up and down. It's nodding, okay?

"Okay, so where is she?"

Dude swivels and swerves, making a gesture as if to

say, "Up that way, dude." Aha. So the master bedroom. Probably hiding in the closet or barricaded in. Okie dokie, let's go make that money.

I take the stairs four at a time. The floorboards are creaky as hell, so I know she hears me now. Here I come, baby. I march to the end of the hall, *creak creak creeeaak,* reach the door to the master bedroom. I try the doorknob. Locked. Tee-hee, I just love the desperation. Like oh yeah, locking the door is gonna stop me. I give it a shove and easily force it open.

A precious little whimpering is coming from the closet. She's trying so hard to be quiet, bless her soul. I come closer, walk right up to the double-folding closet doors. More whimpering, hyperventilating. Sorry, sweetie. It's just impossible to control your breathing when you're in a state of panic and fear.

I rip open the closet doors.

Noelle lets out a tiny, terrified squeak from somewhere in there. I reach in and sweep all the clothes on hangers out of the way, then continue digging. It only takes a second to find her, all huddled in the corner under a couple suitcases, hats and shoes, hoping I won't see her buried under all that rubble. Sorry, honey.

"Hi," I say, giving her a friendly wave.

"No! No, please!" She's not happy to see me.

I reach in to grab her, and that's when she whips out the knife. All I see is a quick flash of metal, then I feel that fucker impaling my hand. Fuck! It's one of those big kitchen knives and the first three inches of it are poking through the back of my hand. And in case I need to make this clear, it fucking hurts.

I hiss and stumble back, and little Alice in Wonderland is already yanking her knife back out and scrambling away. I grip my bleeding hand, not sure if I want to check out my new wound or keep my eye on the little lamb running out the bedroom door. Shit. I go after her.

The hooked machete is in my right hand and my left hand is dribbling blood. By the time I reach the top of the stairs I see her booking it through the living room, screaming of course, and out the back door. Shit! I run down the stairs and chase after her.

I see her running into the backyard and around the pool. I have a shot. I take it. *Whoosh*, I launch the machete across the backyard, spinning its way to the target... *Whack!* It stabs Noelle right in the lower back! Yes!

She makes a little grunt sound, stumbles, falls right into the bubbling jacuzzi. Oooooh, I was hoping for an excuse to get me some bubbles! I walk on over, watching her thrash around in a dumb-fuck panic. It's so funny, she looks retarded.

So I step on in—Ooooh! That's hot!—and reach down to pull Noelle's head up out of the water. Don't want you to die just yet, sweetheart. First, I have some questions.

"What's your name?"

Noelle coughs and sputters water. She's in shock, her whole body's probably lit up with pain thanks to that big, flat blade sticking out of her spine. I shake her a little and ask again. She looks up at me, scared and confused.

"Yoo hoo, Noelle! Can you hear me?" I look closer, wondering if she can even answer questions at this point or if I should just stop wasting time and rip this bitch in half already. She's blinking, seems like she's still conscious.

"Where are you from?" I try that.

"W-what happened...?" she whispers, looks delirious.

"You're dyin'," I say. "Where are you from? What are your hobbies? Tell me somethin' interestin' about yourself."

"...Huh?"

"Come on, Noelle. Tell me about yourself."

"W-why do you keep calling me Noelle?"

What was that? Now I'm on to something. I pull her in closer.

"Your name's not Noelle?"

"My name's Katie... What happened? H-how did I get here?" She starts to cry. It's pathetic. "W-who are you? What am I d-doing here? I-I want my mommy!"

"Katie? That's your name?" I give her a hard shake as I see her start to fade. "Tell me more, Katie. How did you get here?"

Noelle's — or Katie's — eyelids are getting heavy. I'm losing her.

I'm sitting here with her in this hot tub, and it does feel very nice and hot and bubbly, trying to kill this little lamb chop, but also trying to keep her awake just a little bit longer. I didn't plan this out very well. And as if I needed more evidence of that, miss thing surprises me yet again.

Turns out she's still holding on to that knife, because she whips it out from under the water and stabs me right in the fucking neck. *Gaggk!* Oh fuck, I feel every inch of that cold, stainless steel cutting through my throat, all the muscles and blood vessels, scraping across my spine.

I drop the bitch down into the jacuzzi as I fall back, gripping my throat. The fucking knife is jammed in there good, so I yank it out. That was a mistake. Now the whole thing is hemor-hemirg- it's bleeding a fucking lot. I feel myself getting light-headed, going cold. I collapse onto the patio between the jacuzzi and the pool, spewing blood everywhere.

I'm dying! Shit! I look back at Noelle, Katie, whatever her name is, and it looks like she's still gripping the edge of the whirlpool, still trying to pull herself out. Come on, Marvin! Stay alive just another minute, just long enough to finish her off!

I struggle to pull myself up but the lights are going out. My arms and legs are cold and numb. I'm fading. Fuck. I'm dead.

CHAPTER 17

I WAKE up lying on the stage floor back at the Grand Malavista Arena.

Harsh lights are in my eyes. The fans are screaming. My wounds are gone. Hoo, that's a relief. That shit hurt. Still, I'm frustrated. I was so close to finishing the deal. Now I have to go back in *again*, ugh.

I stand up and Jim runs up to greet me with the other boys. But David Black is coming out onto the stage too, along with Bruno Bivens, some of ring officials, and a beefy security team. Hm, don't know what they're up to. The clash ain't over yet, no reason for anyone to be coming on stage.

Jim looks a little embarrassed, maybe even worried.

"You okay?" I ask.

"Sure, man. Sure," Jim says, handing me a towel and a water.

"What's wrong?" I ask. "I got plenty of time on the clock and I can get killed two more times. There's nothin' to worry about, man. This last chick is already half dead."

"Yyyyeah..." Jim looks like he's trying to tell me something.

Mr. Black, Bruno, and this official-looking guy talk amongst themselves, then finally, Bruno takes center stage and holds up his mic to speak.

"Ladies and gentlemen, after two periods of mayhem,

Judges Brian J. Karsch and Derek Seldeen, as well as chairman of the Malavista Athletic Commission, Christopher P. Genovese, and BMC president David Black, have come to a decision," Bruno clears his throat. "Unfortunately, due to several penalties and code violations, Marvin Brumlow has been disqualified at this time..."

My eyes go wide. My heart stops. *What?*

The crowd goes berserk, screaming and throwing things at the stage.

"What?!" I demand, stomping forward to get in Mr. Black's face. But he's surrounded by a wall of suits with guns. I turn to look at Jim and he's hanging his head. "Jim, what the fuck?!"

"They tried to tell you, dude," he says, "the rules are very strict."

"What the..." I push against the bodyguards, but as big as I am, there's a lot of them. "Mr. Black! What the fuck, man? I still have time on the clock! Let me get back in there and finish this!"

David Black looks at me, disappointed. "Forget it, Marvin."

I look at the commentary booth, and Larry is sitting there shaking his head at me. I look around at the other faces in the crowd, and it looks like there might be a riot. Some people seem pissed at me, others seem pissed at the BMC. Everyone is pissed.

"According to chairman Genovese of the Malavista Athletic Commission, Mr. Brumlow is in violation of two counts of BMC code 127, illegal use of psychological manipulation and leading the victim, and one count of BMC code 16, unauthorized use of aerial photography equipment. All kills from this clash will be stricken from Mr. Brumlow's record, his purse withheld, and he is as of now under suspension until further notice."

"Motherfucker!" I lunge at David Black but his gang of goons hold me at bay. "What are you tryin' to hide, *David*? Who are these kids really? Huh?" But the bald man in the black suit just shakes his head at me and walks away. I try to push through his goons, but I'm not super strong here in Hell. Yeah, I'm still a huge, strong guy here, but during a clash I can bench-press a fucking Buick.

So now I'm being pushed away and I'm just in shock. Even Jim is pulling gently at my arm, trying to be sympathetic. I mean, he's still smacking away at that fucking gum nonstop — that never changes — but he does seem to actualy feel bad right now. The fans are also pissed. Did I just give them all a glimpse behind the curtain, show them something they're not supposed to see?

"Come on, bro," Jim says, pulling me away. "Fuck those guys."

I let him and the other boys in my corner team lead me back to the dressing room. A team of six big — not as big as me, of course — security dudes follow me every step of the way. I change out of my bloody clothes, shower, put on a fresh track suit, and they're on me like glue. Bastards. Yes, I'm leaving. I'm going home, having a drink, probably watching some French porn, and going to sleep.

But I won't forget this. I have to get to the bottom of it.

. . .

Okay, maybe this isn't the best idea.

It's two days after the clash. I'm crouched in the bushes outside David Black's house. It's the middle of the night. This community makes Beverly Hills look like Skid Row. The house is a fucking castle, and there's a few of those black-suit-security fuckers patrolling the grounds. With guns.

I'm either crazy or stupid or both. This isn't a clash. I'm "alive" in Hell right now, and if I get myself killed, I don't just get two more tries like a fucking video game. If one of these goons pumps me full of lead and I die... that's it. I'll be sent down to the next level of Hell, whatever that is. It's not like anyone who goes there ever comes back. But I don't care. Nobody does me like that, *Mister* Black. Nobody.

I'm gonna get the truth if I have to pull it out of your ass.

I brought my new hooked machete and another big fucking knife.

My game plan for this is simple: No subtlety or stealth at all. I stand up, hop over the wall, and land in David Black's backyard. Oooh, nice. Big pool, waterfall, a jacuzzi that puts the last one to shame. Pacing around near one of the back doors is a security bro with what looks like an Mp5? Wait, let me look closer... Yep, that's an Mp5. Nice.

I move quick, rushing at him. I cover ground fast, raising my big chopper. The guard turns, sees me coming, eyes go wide, he starts to turn and aim — *Schlotthzssh!!* I take off the top two-thirds of his head in a rad, sloped angle, looks pretty cool. He staggers and falls and, naturally, I scoop up the Mp5.

"Breach! Breach!" I hear someone screaming.

They're on to me. Good.

I kick the back door in, aiming the compact little mini-gun, and charge inside. Two goons are already coming at me, raising their sights. Nope, I'm quicker. I just squeeze that trigger as I run ahead. *BRRTTT-TAATATATAATT!!!*

They both fall and choke on blood and die. And now I'm empty.

I throw the gun aside and stalk through the kitchen. Wow, this really is something, this place is a palace! While I'm busy being a stupid tourist and enjoying the view, another muscle-head comes around a corner, opening fire at me.

The bullets hit the marble countertop nearby, and little chips and shards of marble fly at me, cutting in. I duck behind a pillar and take out the smaller of my two knives. I see the goon charging in, so I spin and whip the knife out... *Chufft!!*

The blade lodges balls-deep right in his fucking chest. Macho Man falls to his knees, sputtering and choking on blood. I step in, grab the handle of the knife, and give it a good-hard twist as I pull it out. This of course causes way more damage and is really a terrible way to die. Hee-hee.

Three more douchebags come at me from different angles, shooting wildly. One round clips my forearm! Fuck! Another one rips through my overalls, barely missing my chest. I take the blood-soaked knife and charge at the first guy, digging it into his gut and lifting him high over my head.

"*AAAIIIIEEEEE!!! HEEEEEELP!!!*"

I take this little squirrel and throw him at his friends. They collapse into a pile of blood and guts like some morbid Three Stooges routine and it gives me a good laugh. As the two remaining guys struggle to get back to their feet, I step in with the big blade and *SHUNK!!* chop the first guy's arm off at the shoulder. He screams and howls with a real nice tone as he gushes goo. I spin and jam the hook-end of the machete into his belly button, then rip up and split him open like a frog.

He falls down dead. The last of them screams, trying to aim his gun, but I'm quicker. With one good *swish* I chop his head clean off. His body falls, convulsing in death as the gaping wound bleeds out.

I take his head and stuff it nose-first into his own ass.

"Happy now, Marvin?" It's David Black.

I turn and see him standing at the foot of the stairs in a black, silk robe. Big surprise. I snarl and stomp towards him, gripping my machete tight.

"Start talkin', David," I say, dripping with his men's blood.

"You really have some balls, Marvin. You really do."

"Start talkin'!" I scream.

"Or what? Huh? What are you gonna do?"

"Look here you little—" I go to grab him and my body suddenly seizes up. I fall to the floor, convulsing in pain, unable to move a damn muscle.

"You really need to learn to read your contracts, Marvin. You can't hurt me, any more than you can hurt your manager or any other official of the BMC." He comes closer, confident as he circles me.

"W-what's goin' on here, damn it?" I'm convulsing on the floor, helplessly screaming up at him. "Who are these kids? Are they even real? Is the Boogeyman Championships all some virtual reality, computer thing? Is this whole thing just in my mind? *What the hell is goin' on here?*"

He shakes his head and snorts.

"Well, since you asked so nicely, Marvin... You want to know what's going on behind the curtain? Fine." He kneels down and looks at me. My body stops convulsing and I can finally relax. "No, it's not in your head, and it's not a video game. It's real, Marvin."

"Then why does it seem so fake? Why do these kids look like they'd never actually be friends? Why do some of these kids look like they're thirty-five years old? Why are some of them rememberin' different names?"

"They're all real people, Marvin. All flesh and blood. But they're not who you think they are. They're not even who *they* think they are. They're young people we find from all over the U.S. Mostly homeless people, drifters, prostitutes, runaways. People who won't be missed. So we scoop them up, do a little 'reprogramming' and presto. They're now someone new entirely with fake memories, for us to use as we see fit. They're pieces on a chess board, Marvin."

"B-but why...?"

"Let's say we have you go in and kill a group of actual friends. These people all know each other, all live in the same place. That makes headlines. The BMC doesn't like headlines. But if we take a runaway from Wisconsin, a druggie from New York, a hooker working the highways... We give them new memories, new identities. Then when drop them in a completely neutral place for the clash. That way, the authorities on Earth can't track any of it.

And remember, it's not just you, Marvin. We have a lot of other Boogeymen on our roster. Imagine if every time one of our boys did a clash, a small group of real friends in some remote location gets chopped to bits! That would be a big pattern, and that's the kind of thing that causes trouble even 'down here' in Malavista. So, we take lost souls who are essentially already missing, do what we want with them, then clean the site completely afterwards so it's like it never happened. Does that make sense, Marvin?"

I nod, my mind spinning.

"Good. Then understand this. What I should do right now, what I want to do, is to blow your fucking head off. You break into my home, murder my entire security team? Many of whom were my *friends?* Look what you did to Kenny!! You fucking *bastard. Fuck you...*" he takes a deep breath, trying to control his anger. "But it just so happens that the numbers for your last clash were the second-highest in BMC history. People just seem to love you, you *fuck.*"

"So, what are you sayin' to me?" I ask.

"I'm saying that if I want my business to continue to profit, I need to keep you around. People want to see you keep killing. So you're going to keep killing, and making me money. Got it? Good."

I stand up slowly, humbled. I look around at the

carnage I've caused. The entire house is fucked, bullet holes in the walls, furniture smashed, blood and guts and corpses everywhere. Shit, now I feel bad.

"S-sorry," I shrug.

"Fuck you, Marvin."

"Okay, well..." I shift from foot to foot, feeling awkward. "I guess I'll go now. Sorry..." I start to back away.

"Um, excuse me?" he says, his eyebrows furrowing. "You're not going anywhere until you help me clean up this mess!"

I survey the damage. Shit.

It's gonna be a long night.

To be continued...

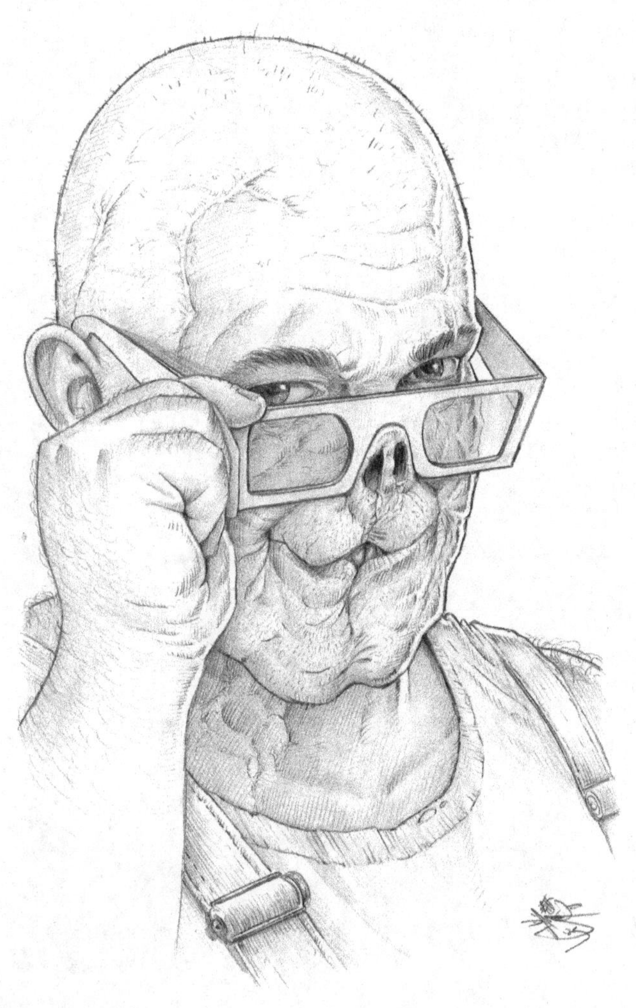

Jesse D'Angelo is an author and illustrator, born in New York, raised in California, and currently residing in Georgia with his wife and son. He is a veteran of the film and television industries and has also worked with law enforcement as a sketch artist on multiple criminal investigations.

When not writing books about horrible monsters and brutal serial killers, he spends his time changing diapers, scooping cat litter, and trying to avoid other human beings to the best of his ability.

ALSO BY THE AUTHOR

Lady of the Lake

Prey To God

A Collection of Tails

Skinner

Blackbirds Dance

Composite

Doomsday Dogs

Dying Sheep

Dying Sheep 2

9 781966 037491